The Education of
Chauncey Doolittle

Books by James Everett Kibler

The Education of Chauncey Doolittle
Memory's Keep
Walking Toward Home
Child to the Waters
Our Fathers' Fields: A Southern Story

The Education of Chauncey Doolittle

JAMES EVERETT KIBLER

PELICAN PUBLISHING COMPANY
Gretna 2009

Library of Congress Cataloging-in-Publication Data

Kibler, James E.
  The education of Chauncey Doolittle / James Everett Kibler.
    p. cm.
  ISBN 978-1-58980-634-4 (alk. paper)
  1. South Carolina--Fiction. I. Title.
  PS3611.I26E38 2009
  813'.6--dc22

                          2009005445

This is a work of fiction. Any resemblance to actual persons is
coincidental.

Printed in the United States of America
Published by Pelican Publishing Company, Inc.
1000 Burmaster Street, Gretna, Louisiana 70053

Dedicated, with thanks, to
Bannie Kennedy, Billy Hendrix, Val Green,
Ronnie Abrams, and Ward Allen
storytellers of the old school

Contents

The Education of Chauncey Doolittle

An essential of a man's life, if he wishes to rediscover a contact with the world outside him, is not mobility, but position.
—T. H. White

Merchants have no country. The mere spot they stand on does not constitute so strong an attachment as that from which they draw their gains.
—Thomas Jefferson

I
In a New Season

The tall farmhouse was built on the compass point to face east. It was two centuries old now and was a single room deep. The sun came up in the front windows and set in the rear. The four-poster bed in Chauncey's bedroom on the second floor had its headboard against the room's western wall so that the sun's first rays would strike startlingly full on his face, that is, if it ever had the chance. It seldom did. The gentle greying was enough to stir Chauncey's blood to activity. Such a rude late awakening was reserved for someone who'd sleep till seven or eight, or, in less happier places, be shocked into the swirl of the day by the shrill alarm of a digital machine.

This bright morning, Chauncey woke with the words of one of his favourite poems. "Sunlit pallets never thrive," he said aloud as he wheeled his legs to the bed's edge. "Clay lies still, but blood's a rover. Breath's a ware that will not keep."

That about summed it up this clear winter day. After so many years of living with the loss of his young wife, he no longer wore his grief like a heavy coat. Chauncey glanced at the calendar. 12 January 2007.

Breakfast was an easy matter. Stone-ground grits from Boykin Mill cooked with cream, home-churned butter, range-fed eggs taken from the nest yesterday, homemade fig preserves to put on his toast, hot chocolate to warm him up. He had to drive a piece over to Boykin to get the grits, but he made the trip only twice a year and bought enough to last. Not having food with preservatives was worth the trip, and then he could visit with Miss Alice the owner and her miller, the latter a poet of no small satiric skill. They always had plenty to talk about.

Today, after breakfast, chores, and half a day's work, he was on his way to make one of his rare visits to Clay Bank. He was driving Blue Bessie, his beat-up Ford pickup. As he got near town and the road widened, traffic flew by him both ways. He still tried to give his friendly steering wheel waves but soon gave up with all the dizzying blur. Instead, he fell deep in thought about this or that, maybe his collards that needed cutting, or the tomato seeds he needed to be starting in the greenhouse, or the ploughing of another acre or two of winter fields to let the soil breathe in advance of spring.

At a bend of the road, he noticed a tall figure walking his way, coming out of town with a powerful long stride that signified business. The walker looked like he wanted to get away something fierce.

"Well, look at that," Chauncey said.

He could tell Trig Tinsley's stride a mile away. He and Trig had grown up together but hadn't been close back then. Their fathers were, however, hunting and fishing together, sharing harvesting chores and butcherings, helping each other out on their farms when things were tight, as often they were. Both their fathers had taught their sons the same definition of thrift—making do with what your granddaddy passed down—and this was a bond that had drawn the two together, that and a lot of similar ways of looking at things.

As Blue Bessie idled, Trig slowed too. He'd recognized the truck from the sound of the motor even before she'd turned the curve and come into view.

Chauncey could tell from the determined slant of his friend's head that, yes, today, he was mightily determined about something.

A stream of cars whizzed by, barely slowing, as Chauncey pulled off the road onto the shoulder. He greeted his friend. Chauncey knew from Trig's looks that he'd probably have a tale to tell and that the story would likely be worth sacrificing the errands he had to do in town.

So he decided to turn around and give Trig a lift home. It wasn't but a few miles to Trig's farmhouse, but this would be the excuse to visit awhile. These last years, he'd come to value their friendship as among his most prized possessions. And Trig's stories were always worth whatever trouble you'd have to hear them. Chauncey had gradually learned to appreciate their community wisdom, he could get few places else in quite so natural and enjoyable a way.

Trig willingly obliged. For truly he had the gift of gab. Blarney was too tame a term for it.

"Well, Chauncey," he said as he got in.

"Well, Trig," Chauncey replied.

But Triggerfoot didn't have his usual broad smile. Instead, he ran his fingers through the shock of curly hair, still coppery blond at his age, his youthful looks belying his years. Around his ears was the first light frosting of silver.

"I be damned!" he began after settling down a little. "Dang if I ain't been gotten the best of today. In my lifetime, I've swam the Broad River with a broke arm, stared a bobcat in the eye, and caught hold of a panther's tail. I've kept warm a-winter from climbing a pine tree and sliding down. When I'm up to it, I can out-beller thunder and have been known to ride on a tornado. When I get thirsty, the river hides. But today, Chaunts, I've just been wiped up all but a smear, and now I'm on the run. Can't get away from Clay Bank quick enough. Just see how I'm sweatin', and on a cold day."

"Fleeing from justice, no doubt," Chauncey answered in a way that would get to the tale faster than would be the usual wont of easing there by meanderings—for which in storytelling, Trig was the expert and master complete. His tales were circling knots, woven to perfection into a satisfying whole, whose design you couldn't see at first until you backed off far enough. Chauncey surmised his way of telling owed a lot to his ancestral Irish genes.

"The sheriff after you again? Or is it one of them wild Clay Bank women trying to settle you down?"

"No, it's worse than all that and more. I can handle the sheriff. He's only the law. And as for women, getting caught's not the worse thing in the world. No, it's a heap more." Trig answered without his usual pause. "I'm not fleeing from justice, or injustice neither. I'm running from Doc Clarence and his mule pliers."

"Why, what's he after you for?"

Old Doc Clarence McCracken Renwick was the super-annuated dentist in town. He had a one-room dental office up above the old post office building on Main Street, where sat his one dental chair, the first the town had ever seen. It was still there, as was old Doc. Doc Clarence had used it for over sixty years, and he was still the only dentist in town. The post office had moved long ago to one of the strip malls on the edge of the sprawl.

Doc's drill ran so slow it made the most hideous sounds, almost as horrible as the sounds from struggling patients who gripped white knuckled the arms of the dental chair. The heat from the slow drill really played hell with the nerves. Nothing closer to the iron maiden or the various medieval machines of torture could be imagined. For all the world, it looked to Triggerfoot like an electric chair, ready for the execution of dam-fools such as himself who'd let their heads be pressed against those little adjustable pads.

As for Doc Clarence, he was now in his eighties; but despite his age, he still had a firm enough hand, that is, whenever he was sober, for, as everyone knew, he loved his dram.

Many times, it was considerably more than a dram, or

even a couple of toddies, the town also knew. In the old days, it had always been said of him that if he got dry and his daddy was drowning, he'd go to the liquor gourd before he'd go to his pa.

If you got the good Doc on a sober day you were like to be partly okay, but if you got him on a bad one, then, well . . .

So Trig had just gotten him on one of the bad ones. Under other circumstances, Trig would never have thought of darkening the Doc's door, but he was desperate. And the day wasn't a bad one to start with, but upon that hinged Trig's tale.

Trig had an embedded wisdom tooth, and it had most likely abscessed. It was causing him such trouble that he couldn't even rest, not to mention sleep. It was giving him fever and running him down. This had gone on for nearly two weeks.

As Trig declared, he couldn't have that. He had a farm to take care of and work to do. He tried everything. Mouth-deadening herbs like bark from the toothache tree, remedies from the old days, and new stuff from the drugstore that didn't work as well as the herbs. If he'd been able to get his big hands that far back in his mouth, he'd have pulled it himself. For that was his way. A doc was his very last resort, and when he went, you'd know he had to.

Now Doc Renwick didn't believe in anesthesia, and he'd never even heard of laughing gas. Doc's patients knew that if they wanted to stop pain, they'd have to resort to their own particular means.

At that, Trig knew exactly what to do. Short-term pain,

he could handle with his jug. He filled him a magnanimous half-gallon of his best and put it under his jacket as he walked into town.

When he got to the dentist, old Doc was sitting in the dental chair reading his *Field & Stream*. He had on his neat, white, starched dentist's coat and was sober as a judge, in fact, soberer than some.

"Just give me a minute," Trig had said to him and quickly drank about a quarter of his jug. He'd imbibed another quarter on his walk into town. "Aaah," Trig sighed, wiping his mouth with the back of his hand.

Doc watched him funnel it down with a hungry look in his eye. "Right then, I should have known," Triggerfoot declared. "Dam-fool me, to drink whiskey in front of old Doc."

The effects of the whiskey came on fast, and Trig felt no pain. He was at peace and happy with everyone in the world. He was seated blissfully in the white porcelain chair, his head on the pads, and his arms on the armrests as comfortable as you please.

But through the haze, he remembered he'd said obligingly, "Sure, Doc, just help yourself."

Then it dawned on him to what he'd agreed. Doc had said, "Let me sample the rest of that," and it was to that request he'd complied.

Through the fog of blurred vision, Trig watched Doc's Adam's apple go gluckgluck chugchug. Then he wiped his lips and was through. He'd tossed off the contents as quick as a blink.

Doc's hands, they were steady enough, but his vision must have been muddled, for after a mighty struggle of pulling, Trig's body holding itself braced down in the chair, Doc pulled the wrong tooth.

Trig wasn't quite inebriated enough not to know that. In fact, as it was happening, he thought he figured what tooth was what, but since his mouth was crammed full of cotton, Doc's hand, and his dental equipment, he couldn't communicate. Old Doc took Trig's struggles and mumblings and thrashings for normal reactions to what was happening in his mouth. He'd seen plenty of that before.

So out at last came the wrong tooth!

"Doc, hell!" Trig half mumbled, half shouted through wads of cotton and blood. "You pulled a good one. That'un you got in the pliers ain't the one that's bad."

"Well, what about that! But don't you worry none, son. I'll get the right one this time." He had one hand on Trig's shoulder holding him down, and the other trying to pry open Trig's bloody mouth.

But Trig was out of there lots faster than he'd come in, much quicker than he'd believed he could move under any circumstances anywhere. He said he made better time than if the building was burning down.

Last glimpse as he turned the corner of the hall was Doc still standing in his little white coat with his hands full of tools and humming a tune.

"A funeral tune," said Trig. "In respect to the recently departed—just dam-fool me."

Triggerfoot picked up the thread of his narrative: "The liquor had worn clean off as I hit the stairs, or maybe the skeer had sobered me up. But I was clear-headed as ever I've been. And my bad tooth was still hurting like hell. So this is why you see me making fast tracks out of town. Don't want to go back to Clay Bank as long as I live!"

"But Trig, what about the pain in your tooth?"

"Reckon, against my wishes and good judgement, I might have to go back another day, but this time for certain I'll drink up my dram and Doc's too before I come up his stairs. Lord, Chauncey, I sure dread to even think of going back anywhere near that town. All I can see is old Doc in that little white operating coat and his electric chair. Dang if I can get him out of my head."

Chauncey helped Trig do his farm chores, and then took him on home with him. Chauncey put him to bed in the spare room, with a spittoon for his pulled tooth, some pretty good pain pills, and some antibiotics he had on hand, left over from when he'd stepped on a nail last summer.

Tomorrow, he'd take Trig up to his dentist friend in Spartanburg. Yes, that's what he'd do.

He cleaned up the kitchen and went to bed, then lay there in the dark, thinking over the day.

Trig's one of God's special own, he smiled, and besides, he makes the smoothest liquor I ever sipped down. Can't take any risks of wasting such a man. Got to look out for old Trig.

Chauncey let his mind wander over all that he and Trig had been through over the years. He recalled some of the quiet truths he'd learned from him, lessons that loomed larger as the years passed. He reviewed them in succession as he drifted off to an untroubled sleep.

II
Odyssey

~⟋☙⟍~

Next morning Chauncey did his chores, scraped the frost off his windshield, and drove Trig down to his farm at 7:00 to help him with his chores. The brisk cold had the effect of enlivening them both. Then they were on their way to Spartanburg. The dentist, Hardy Rogers, had come from their own community. He was old Jackson Rogers' third son. The Rogers farm, while a good one, wasn't big enough for six children and their families to make a living from, so Hardy went off to college and dental school, and then to practice in town.

He and Chauncey were the same age. They'd been friends as lads and even together in college for the full four years. They'd double-dated a few times, and Rogers had married one of Chauncey's distant cousins from Clay Bank. When Rogers had first gone to Spartanburg, Chauncey had really missed him.

Trig's appointment wasn't until ten, so instead of taking the interstate, Chauncey decided to go the old way. On this route, they'd have a chance to look at pastures, the condition of orchards, maybe see how the winter gardens were doing this time of year.

"Somebody's had them some cowpeas and collards for New Year's," Trig said as he observed a clean-picked pea field and gaps in the neat rows of a farmer's collard patch. The stubs of half a dozen plants from which the tops had been cut looked to him like the stumps of teeth.

"Good-looking collards," Chauncey added. "They must have gotten hold of Bo Bowers' collard seed. Some must be a full three feet across."

"Fine-looking turnip greens too," Trig said. "And broad-leaf mustard greens."

There was a pause in the conversation as they drove along. They passed a farmer in a freshly ploughed row drilling seed. He looked up and waved at them as they drove by.

Around the curve, the road came right beside a white wooden fence. Several sleek, well-fed horses grazed inside. One spirited black ran up to the fence, snorted, then wheeled. The rippling play of his thin glossy coat revealed muscles and veins. The two men were so close that they could hear him and see the look of unbridled freedom burning in his eyes.

"Feeling his oats," Trig observed. They rode on.

"Look at those fat Guernseys," Chauncey said a piece up the road, nodding his head toward a cluster of cows by a willow-lined creek. "My grandmother always said she liked Guernseys the best. And she knew her cows."

"Fine cream there," Trig replied. "Like nothing you can get in plastic jugs and cans."

He paused. "Reminds me of Old Missus Bat Carroll, who entered that condensed-milk contest back when canned milk was first beginning to be used. She heard an ad on the radio saying five thousand dollars for the best slogan. Only rule was the rhyme had to begin with 'Canned milk is best of all.' Pa told me that Old Missus Carroll said, 'I know all about milk and cows, been working with them since I was old enough to walk and carry a pail. I can do this.' So she wrote off her rhyme about canned milk."

"Seems like I remember my mama saying something about that too," Chauncey said. "She won, didn't she?"

"Nope. She lost. But a fancy car drove up in her yard, a man wearing a pinstriped suit got out, and gave her a check for a thousand dollars. Most money she'd ever seen, and probably saved the farm. The canned-milk man told her, 'Sorry. We ain't able to use your rhyme, Ma'am, but we loved it, and it should have won.' I still remember her lines:

> *Canned milk is best of all.*
> *No tits to pull, no hay to haul.*
> *No buckets to wash, no shit to pitch.*
> *Just poke a hole in the son-of-a-bitch.*

Now ain't canned milk about as efficient as modern times can get?"

Chauncey agreed and laughed at his friend. Trig laughed

too but stopped short and said, "Ow." He put the back of his hand to his jaw. "Ow, ow," he repeated. "Holy hell."

Chauncey changed the subject as a way to get Trig's mind off his trouble. He'd gotten interested in reading William Faulkner over Christmas. A cousin in Columbia had given him an American Library collection of six novels, and he'd already finished two. He'd really liked the one called *The Hamlet.* The place where it was set sounded a lot like his and Trig's world. He knew a few folks like Flem Snopes, but they were mostly in town behind cash registers. "Like Warn Pulliam," Trig volunteered. Ratliff was Chauncey's favourite character in the novel, a born storyteller like Trig and Kildee. In fact, Ratliff reminded him a lot of his friends in a number of ways. "I'd sure like to meet that Eula Varner," he'd said as he finished the last page.

The cousin who sent him the present also gave him an appropriate story to go with the book. So to get Trig's mind off his ordeal, Chauncey passed the tale along to him. He narrated at ease. They had plenty of time.

Trig was a ready listener. "Them pain killers of yours have kicked in again and have got me relaxed for a tale," he declared.

The anecdote was a true story that concerned one of Faulkner's own kin. The cousin who'd given Chauncey the book had an in-law in Columbus, Mississippi, whose own cousin's father had been one of the young men in the story. The old gentleman in the story was one of Faulkner's kin.

"Yep," Chauncey said as he began his narrative. "I can

believe every word of that tale. My cousin told me that Mr. Faulkner, the writer I told you I been reading this Christmas, had an old atheist uncle. He was a bachelor like us and lived at the Gilmer Hotel. My cousin says people in Columbus have now torn the old building down, but back then in the '20s it was a hopping place.

"The old fellow took his meals there in the hotel dining room. He sat in the lobby and read the papers each and every morning. In the evening, he'd dress up in a white linen suit and sit there again and be on hand to go where fate opened a door. While everybody else went to church on Sundays, he sat in the lobby and was the first at the table when the Gilmer dining room opened at one."

"Not a perfect life," Trig interrupted. "But I can think of worse."

"One evening, some boys, including one of my cousins, were out driving a new T-Model Ford, and picked the old fellow up. They were headed for a bootlegger's place in the hills just over the Alabama line. 'Just wait till I get my hat,' he'd said. Day or night, he didn't go anywhere without his panama.

"Up the long incline, the T-Model went, bright lights working off the generator, lighting up the whole countryside, waking dogs, bringing folks to windows and doors, and frightening cows and horses out in the night fields. The men hollered and sang.

"They drank whiskey, lots of it, bought some to take back, drank some more from Ball jars on their way home.

"Down the hill they raced, getting faster as they went. Generator not pulling, lights getting dimmer and dimmer, then out. Only a sliver of moon, then clouds, no moon at all.

"The driver was brave and powered by his own brand of fuel, sort of like your bravery in Doc Clarence's chair."

No comment from Trig.

"In the pitch dark, weaving from side to side of the rutted road, jolting everybody as he crossed the ruts, spilling and sloshing the whiskey from the jars, the driver was singing to the top of his lungs, Polly wolly doodle all the day. Getting faster and faster down the long incline.

"Faulkner's uncle, now really scared for certain, prayed out loud over the commotion and the rush of wind round the flimsy shield, Lord, you know I haven't bothered you in sixty years. If you'll just get me back to the Gilmer Hotel in Columbus, Mississippi, I promise never to bother you again.

"When they got back to Columbus, the old fellow realised his hat was gone. Had blown off some time in the wild ride, and he'd not even known. He marched through the lobby without saying a word and went straight to bed."

They were nearing Spartanburg. You could tell from the dotting of big houses being built on the hillsides back from the road, huge two- and three-story affairs of brick and stone; their big yards still bare or raw. McMansions Chauncey called them. Trig noted that they were plopped down in the middle of what use to be pastures, peach orchards, or fields. McMansions in a McWorld, and with no regard to the landscape around. "Look at me," the mansions seemed to say. Chauncey vowed it was going to take nothing short of a depression to end all that. "Or there won't be an inch of farmed soil left," he declared.

Trig agreed.

They were on Pine Street now, entering town. The dentist's office was a few blocks away. The jumble of houses, parking lots, storefronts, and signs advertising various services and wares passed smoothly in blur to either side.

After a pause, Trig looked at his friend. "Don't believe I've ever met an atheist," he said.

"Plenty of them around," answered Chauncey. "In church and out. Especially in cities and colleges. Science, degrees, power, and money always seem to collide with God. And men who think they're on the top of the heap and can manage everything seem to congregate in places like that. Not so many around where we live. Leastways they never tell. Bad for business and getting elected to office."

"Got to be an ache with the atheist that's worse than my tooth with none of your magic pills. Guess what they needs is a quart of bootleg, a scarey T-Model ride in the pitch dark, or a doctor like Clarence with his mule pliers to wake up their souls."

"Some such cataclysm at least," Chauncey replied.

Chauncey drove his truck into the parking lot among Land Rovers, BMWs, and SUVs, and the two friends went inside. They could hear the sound of a dental drill from a room somewhere down the long white hall. It was 9:45.

If Rogers could spare it in his rushed routine, Chauncey wanted the space of a few minutes to say hello to his old friend and to catch up on their doings. They hadn't seen each other in over a year. Rogers was always busy and hadn't come their way in quite some time. For him to make space in his schedule for a visit was impossible. His life was more regulated than a traffic light and more regimented than a new army recruit.

At 10:15, Rogers came out rushed. This early in the morning, he was already behind. There had been an emergency. One of his patients had broken a tooth down into the quick and had to be worked in. Chauncey could see the patient in the first room, his mouth packed full of rubber and cotton, and the bright light focused down on his open mouth. Clamps held his lips stretched wide. Only his eyes moved. They were staring wide. He was inhaling hard on the nitrous oxide, waiting for Rogers to return.

A handshake was about all Chauncey and Rogers had time for, and Trig was whisked efficiently away by a pretty young dental assistant and placed far down the hall in room number four. She was prepping him for Rogers to come in and shoot narcotics with a long needle into his gums.

The forced chatter and scatter of rumpled magazines in the waiting room put Chauncey on edge, nervous like those in line to be called. Chauncey noticed some of the titles: *National Geographic, Money Magazine, Forbes, Town & Country.* A man in a business suit was talking to a smartly dressed woman about the recent dip in the stock market. She wondered if now wasn't the time to buy gold. A child next to Chauncey whimpered, jerked hard at the sleeve of his mother's shirt, then cried. Neither toys nor a candy bar could console him.

It was too hot and stuffy in the room and filled with strange smells. He wasn't accustomed to central heat and a temperature this high inside. He'd dressed layered for the January cold as he always did and had his thermals on. He'd taken his jacket off when he entered the office, but this hadn't helped. His forehead was beaded with sweat. The child, unpacified by his plastic toy, threw it across the room, hitting the plastic potted plant with a thud and clatter. His mother pulled him onto the seat with a reprimand.

Chauncey took his jacket from the rack and walked back outside to get some air. He liked the nip of cold in the wind that pricked his nose.

He looked at the asphalt around him, the jumble of telephone and electric poles, and the sea of expensive cars. The steady buzz of traffic and city sounds was all he could hear. They reminded him of the dentist drill or the drone of some huge dynamo. No, better, the yawing sound of chain saws and bulldozers in a clear-cut, noise that always grated on his nerves and put him out of sorts.

"Pine Street," he said. "But where are the pines?" Truth to say, he knew that Spartanburg was less guilty than most cities in this. He'd heard about their project to plant trees.

He got back in his truck, decidedly not in style, expensive, or chic, and waited for Trig. He tried to ignore the maze of frantic cars speeding by.

"Must be going somewhere really important," he thought. "As fast as they're going." He hoped Trig was bearing up well inside.

The noise of a siren startled him. As it neared, it blistered his ears even through the rolled up glass. In the distance, peremptory bells rang, and a freight train rumbled somewhere on its tracks. He could hear its whistle as it signaled warning at the crossings it was passing by. He was sensitive to a multitude of sounds, and sat there trying to pick out where and what they were.

This world was so unlike his own. He had time to think what a blessing silence was, one of the rare free things. His main solace there in the parking lot was knowing that he'd not have to wait long to leave this scene behind and point Blue Bessie south toward home.

III

Ossification: A New Lesson Learned

Chauncey had helped Trig get his bad tooth pulled, and to celebrate their success, they spent the following Saturday afternoon at Kildee Henderson's store. Trig had a good audience this cold winter day and had a tale to tell about an old fellow named Toot-toot Williams. Most of the men gathered there had either known or known of him.

Toot-toot had a real first name, though no one of the assembled knew what it was. No one but Trig, that is. It was Louis, pronounced Louey. The town he toot-tooted through most every day a half-century ago had given him the nickname and had got used to him and his signature sounds announcing that he was passing through. Without a toot-toot day, his superannuated A-Model Ford toot-tooting at everything he passed—people, dogs, lawn jockeys, mailboxes, telephone poles—folks felt something was missing for sure. They couldn't put a finger on just what, but miss something they did.

Some of the more practical-joking, fun-loving men of

Clay Bank, small-time merchants, store clerks, and such, had further nicknamed him Screwy Louey, because it was patently clear to them that he had a screw loose somewhere in his jostled-up toot-toot brain. But never mind them and their talk and their names, old Mr. Toot-toot Screwy Louey Williams toot-tooted on, oblivious of the mirth and joviality that he left in his wake, or the smiles he occasioned when even his name was mentioned around.

Give him credit; Mr. Toot-toot wasn't as screwy as they made him out. He was so shortsighted that at a distance he could hardly see more than a blur. By rights, he shouldn't have been driving at all, and wouldn't be allowed to today, but an A-Model Ford in the 1950s wasn't like to cause much of a cataclysm on a two-lane road even if it crashed, and the damage would have been done to the driver, and, besides, taking such a risk was his call. In those days, those in authority weren't so busily intent on protecting people from themselves even when they didn't want to be.

Today Triggerfoot sat with his brogans up on the shiny stove fender. There'd been a big rain the night before, and Trig's shoes were wet from walking through grass and weeds helping Chauncey with his chores. Kildee had had the same problem and had put on a dry pair of socks. Their wet ones were on a coat hanger above the stove.

"You know, folks," Trig began. "They always called old Mr. Toot-toot Williams 'Screwy Louey,' but I'm thinking they'd got it all wrong. He had a heap of sense. Just put yourself in his place. If I was blind as a bat like him, I'd want the world to know I was driving by. All that toot-tooting is only like riding in the daytime with your high beams on, like city folks do in their Mercedes Benzes—to caution the world you're there. For Mr. Toot-toot, it was the same. It just meant, 'Here I come, and y'all know I can't see, so please watch out and don't run over me.' Running over him wouldn't amount to much more than stepping on a throwed away Co-cola can."

"Reckon you're right, Trig," Chauncey agreed. "Hadn't thought of it that way. Ought to think of it as if we were him. Put ourselves in his place."

"Damn straight, and dang if that's not the way it always ought to be. If we'd start walking in other people's shoes, the world might still have a fighting chance."

Kildee added his usual wise assessment of affairs. "What with all the speed and monster-big vans, trucks, SUVs, and motor homes these days, what chance would an A-Model have in a wreck? It would take someone mighty brave, good sighted or no, to get out for long on the road. I've worked on a many of those old machines in my time. They're as simple as a child's toy. If one of these new heavy, finned shark machines was to hit an A-Model, wouldn't much be left but a rattle and a smear."

"Yes, and old Mr. Louey wouldn't toot-toot no more," Trig added solemnly. "He'd be the smear.

"One day I had to go in to Clay Bank with Pa to the Feed and Seed to get a couple of new plough points. Pa'd worn his others down to nubs. The talk at the feed store was all about Toot-toot."

Triggerfoot, without asking, had listened long enough to get the gist of the tale.

Seems that Mr. Toot-toot, besides regularly tooting at every object he passed, could be counted on like clockwork to stop at the Feed and Seed to use the ramshackle bathroom. No day passed that he didn't have to stop in to take him a whiz as he motored through town.

So several men of the place thought they'd have them some fun off him.

Graham Dawkins got the idea and put it to work. You know back in the '60s they had these life-size colour cardboard likenesses of pretty women that you'd put in your stores. Used for advertising this and that, you'd just stand them up, maybe at a counter, maybe at the door. They'd have a balloon caption saying, "Ooh, ooh, it's so good!"—some such kind of pronouncement from lips of cardboard and glue.

Triggerfoot drank, passed his jar to his friends, and then picked up the tale.

"Well, seems Graham got hold of one of them cutouts, this one a mighty pretty tall leggy gal looked at from behind, and her smiling over her bare shoulder at you. She was dressed in the scantiest mite of little red and white polka-dotted skintight shorts, just enough to hide her behind. Her halter top was only a line on her nekkid back. I'm tellin' you Kildee, she didn't have on enough cloth to wad a rifle good. Advertising some Co-cola product or other kind of frivolous truck. 'Ooh. Ooh. It's so good,' she said, keeping the 'it' real vague and looking like she was just stepping in or out of your bed. You could even hear the bedsprings creak.

"Graham had done put this red-headed girl in the bathroom right smack in front of the commode. He declared that she looked for the world like she was there to use the facility.

"It was easy enough for them to know when to set up the scene, and just exactly when, because Lord, you had plenty warning with Mr. Toot-toot tooting every foot of the way. Yes, indeedy, you could hear old Mr. Toot-toot long time before you saw him, and you could clock off the five minutes it would take him to creak open the old bathroom door.

"So they were ready for him, or that red-headed, scanty panty-clad Co-cola girl was. 'Ooh, ooh, it's so good,' said them skin-tight polka-dotted shorts and long legs and all.

"In comes old Mr. Toot-toot in a hurry, down-zipping his pants, before he'd opened the door. Near blind as he was, he was about ready to commence his whiz before the light hit the red polka-dots of the Co-cola girl.

"Joe-Earl Hardy, Graham's partner in crime, who'd stationed himself outside at a good vantage for viewing the scene, said old Toot-toot wet himself from crotch to heel.

"Backing out, Joe-Earl heard Mr. Toot-toot saying, 'Oh! 'scuse me, Ma'am. 'Scuse me, Ma'am,' as his rear hit the opening door."

"Poor old Mr. Louey," Kildee declared, "But I reckon them boys needed some fun around there. Graham and Joe-Earl were pretty much always at their stand. When the hardware had to close, they found them a new job at the

Wal-Mart that shut the Feed and Seed down. They never shirked or played out sick. They were steady providers, tied mainly to home, and didn't have the free reign to go out on a tear as does Triggerfoot here."

"Tear, smare, Kildee Henderson! I do my share. Ain't no farmer worth the saltpeter in his pee going to shirk no part of a farm. I plough my rows as straight as any around here. I take out my chamber pot as soon before dawn as the best of society. If ole Trig didn't work hard and stay on top of things every living day, he'd be starved and under the ground, be damned if he wouldn't, and you know it too."

"Don't pay any attention to Kildee, Trig. We know that for sure," answered Chauncey. "But as our old friend Chunkey says, you just seem to be freer than everybody else. Free as the wind. That's the impression you give. You've got the free attitude."

"Attitude, smattitude. What's all that talking worth! Hot-toe-mighty-damn, Chauncey, your book talk's come close to ruining you for polite company. Put it straight this a way: I've always worked more than both Graham and Joe-Earl put together times twenty-two. At six, or at seven, they'd go home and leave their work at the store. I take it with me both night and day. They got steady pay at the end of the week in a little brown envelope. I've seen them get it myself and I know. As for me, it's a real adventure each time I get out of bed to know if what I do will give me the wherewithal to eat. No greenbacks in an envelope coming steady to me, tick tock, each Saturday. For breaks in the grind, I've never stooped to using Mr. Toot-toot and his blind old eyes to get me some fun. If I couldn't get it honest, I'd just sit around warming my stool at the cash register and be glum."

"I reckon a lot of folks have worn out many a pants' seat doing that over the years," Chauncey agreed.

"Bet their heinies is as calloused as my hands from the hay rake, pitchfork, and hoe. They works with their heinies. Maybe old Mr. Toot-toot should have found a way to fool them into dropping down their drawers to make fun of them. Seeing calloused butt cheeks, now wouldn't that be fun."

"There's a lot of that calloused butt cheeks going around these days," Kildee added as he arranged some new canned goods on his shelves. He hadn't stopped a moment from the time Trig and Chauncey had come in the store and sat down by the stove. "Calloused butt cheeks is the disease of the day."

"Near epidemic, I'd say," Triggerfoot agreed. "A new kind of plague."

"It's found mostly around office buildings, especially government kinds, and classrooms, and boardrooms, and big universities," Chauncey volunteered.

"Wonder if in those sort of places, they make love to their chairs?" asked farmer Lyman Eppes as he spoke up from the aisle where he'd been listening more or less intently to all that was said. He'd come in quietly about ten minutes ago.

"If they do, their offspring are papers in blue, pink, and yellow triplets to cause all of us sweat and bother and grey hairs before our time," Kildee replied. "The world would do better to have more Toot-toots among us than a passel of those kind of women and men. They eat up the world with their butts and leave nothing but papers in triplicate behind."

"That's why they's so shingle flat butted, I reckon," Triggerfoot observed. "Sitting at desks and their shiney new computers all the day with backs to the world. Or driving their illigant cars. They got no power behind. It's all in big headedness, all in their minds."

"Dangerous. Dangerous," Chauncey declared. "I've been there myself, and I know."

"Well, Chaunts, are you sayin' you're callous butted, or maybe just cal-assed?" Triggerfoot enquired, looking as serious as such a question would allow.

"Bet his behind is like tanned and aged rawhide, cured down with tannin and dressed against weather with Sno-Seal," Kildee laughed.

"Universities and board rooms and offices can surely do that," Chauncey agreed. "But I had the good fortune to escape before ossification set in in earnest."

"Ossification? Assification, don't you mean?" was Triggerfoot's play on the word.

"No. Petrification," Kildee declared. "Well, Chauncey ain't petrified and won't likely ever be. Farming has clean cured him from that curse and disease. Seems his stride nowadays has stretched out about as long as Trig's."

"Well, dearies, hide, stride, or fried, it's about time I de-assify myself from this chair and get to my chores," said Trig in his usual bluff, hardy way as he rose and ambled to the door.

"Wonder if they pronounce it ossify instead of assify in

their big city towers? You know, like potato or potahto, tomato or tomahto—that kind of thing," Mr. Lyman asked as he also rose to bow from the scene.

Chauncey, with some bitterness tinging his usually melodious voice, summed up the discussion and had the last word on this turn of the conversation. "Whatever the way you pronounce it, its root word is still the same, and mind me, greater dam-fool jackasses than old Mr. Screwy Louey had ever been."

"Amen, and y'all have a good evening at home by the fire," said Kildee as he pulled the chain of the light and shut the store for the day. Now that the days were so short and it turned sharply cold the minute the sun went down, he would get some of his chores done early this evening. The sky was looking like it was fixing to be a long winter week ahead that would keep him on the counter stool more than he'd want to be.

IV

Triggerfoot's Great Balloon Hoax

Another week and the usual suspects had again assembled at the store, Trig among them.

Chauncey could tell that he was about as aggravated as when he took flight from Doc Clarence several weeks ago. The problem once again originated in Clay Bank town, as most of his problems usually did. Warn Pulliam, owner of a grocery there, had really crossed the line this time for sure. Trig vowed to Chauncey that he'd seen Warn put his hand on the scales as he weighed produce, causing it to register heavier in his sales to an unsuspecting farmer buying his goods. The man was down on his luck and had a big family to feed.

Trig had suspected Pulliam of this before, but now there was no mistaking. He'd seen it with his own eyes.

Trig liked to give folks the benefit of the doubt. He tried not to have a suspicious mind and convict a man before he proved himself the scoundrel he was. In fact, he actually wanted folks to be better than they usually were. Then when they proved themselves dishonest, hypocritical, or mean, his tolerance ceased, and this was now the case with Pulliam.

Trig put his brogans on the stove's fender. "You know, Chaunts," he began. "If all the merchants and shopkeepers of this world could be as honest and considerate as old Kildee here, then I wouldn't have too much of an argument with them. I reckon I could live with the varmints making nothing with their hands and living off of the sweat of other men that did, because maybe that's the way it's got to be. But when you see that little slight of hand trick of the pinkie finger on the scales and the way Warn's eyes look like nothing's happening and snake-eyed wily—both at the same time—then you know what the arch deceiver himself must've looked like when he tempted our Lord there on the mountainside."

Pulliam's grocery was a filling station, convenience store, general merchandise-and-produce kind of affair there at the edge of Clay Bank town. His customers were mostly small farmers from the outlying areas of the county who could get a little credit for the items they'd need for carrying on their lives—overalls, sugar, coffee and tea, the few canned goods they used, the cuts from the great bolts of cloth to be made into dresses and shirts, cards of buttons, thread, and such, an occasional plug of red man tobacco or two.

Their perch in the world was precarious enough. They struggled and scuffled to survive. Those of them who held on just barely got by; they didn't have much choice but to deal with Warn, for Pulliam, unlike the grocery chains, sold things on time, waiting to settle up when the crops or some manner of long-waited-for check came in.

The least well off of the men would usually wear overalls six days a week till they were worn out. Then they'd call on Warn to buy what they just couldn't raise. Their wives would swap eggs or a chicken, bright crookneck squash, or tomatoes and snap string beans to credit against their bills. Warn didn't pay much in that way, but what else could they do? The grocery chains wouldn't fool with them at all. These got their produce centrally from great distribution warehouses the size of industrial plants, which they resembled, right down to their huge asphalt parking lots. The produce itself came from far away. California was the usual place. No matter that the tomatoes tasted like wet cardboard, or the squash was shrivelled and speckled, or the snap beans no longer snapped. Not even in your wildest dreams could you hope to find okra, leastways okra that wasn't black with bruise.

But what really got Triggerfoot's goat was the high interest Warn would charge and the way he dealt with those of small enough mind, getting away with it too.

"You know old Pap Pitts," Trig told Chauncey. "He was just singing Warn Pulliam's praise to me the other day. 'Mr. Warn,' Pap declared, 'he gives me the best deals. I borrored five dollars from him near four years ago. All I does is pay him a quarter a week; and you know, Mr. Trig, in all them four years, he ain't never asked for that five dollars one single time.' Poor old feeble-minded Pap. He never had a chance with a slick one like Warn."

"Yep," Chauncey agreed. "Warn always has his eye out for

a profit, big or small. Even if it's a penny, I thinks he just gets a kick out of getting the better of someone. You know, he never smiles. Got no sense of humour. Maybe it's because he's so dried-up waspy small. Beating somebody makes him feel big, as big as a shark makes a minnow feel small."

"Or a big hungry black snake to a tree frog," Kildee added.

At that, Triggerfoot shook his head in agreement. "And he pinches that penny till he makes Lincoln squeal. He's so all-fired stingy, he wouldn't give you air in a jug. The kind of man who wouldn't pass gas at your farm 'cause he'd think it might richen your land."

Kildee vowed he understood why the folks all around didn't like merchants or bankers either. "'Cause they've robbed them all," Kildee declared. "And usury's a real Bible-mentioned sin. I heard one fellow come in the store just the other day say such thieving cattle ought to be shot, but they're so downright legal with their dirty business that you never feel quite justified in going after them that way."

Kildee warmed to the topic. "Grandpa always warned that you better never mortgage a foot of your land to the bankers. If you ain't got cash money, don't buy. If times are hard, do without. Whatever you do, don't buy on time. My principle is to never pay interest, he'd laugh and say."

"Sound wisdom for sure," Chauncey added. "My father always said, sit on an apple crate until you can afford a chair. The people round here who've lasted have come through a hundred and fifty years in spite of bankers, and still they're more or less free. They've survived because of character and sacrifice, and sitting on a lot of apple crates."

Kildee shifted on his chair, a cane-bottom one Trig had made. "Or make your own chair, like Trig did this one," he said, giving Trig a nod of his head. "Reckon we've survived because we've known to stick together as families, neighbours, and friends, and pool our own. Take care of our woods and land. No need to wait for some good luck from outside, especially from Columbia or Washington. More than like, they're more the problem than the solution and just get in our way. We cooperate instead of compete, and success or the lack of it is reckoned by how and not how much we get and do."

"Yep. Washington helps about as much as that FEMA did after the big storm in New Orleans three years ago," agreed Chauncey. "Those big agency men actually stopped private folks from helping people out. Some of our folks up here drove down in trucks with water, ice, and canned goods and weren't allowed to get through. FEMA said they were afraid they might be terrorists. Some just had to turn around and come on back home. It was real frustrating. Others just went on in anyway, risking getting jailed for their pains."

The men sadly nodded their heads.

"In the Kingdom of Thingdom," Chauncey continued. "Government rules, but all it seems to be able to do well is start wars and collect taxes. The only time I ain't ever found it slow and inefficient is in getting taxes out of a paycheck."

"No mistake ever made there." Kildee agreed. "Or delay of time either."

Kildee and Chauncey chattered on with such like conversation, but Trig fell into a brown study. He looked to be in deep thought, with his mind far away. His head nodded in what appeared to be an occasional doze.

About half an hour later, the two friends parted from Kildee's store. Chauncey drove off in Blue Bessie, and Triggerfoot, still silent, went off on foot in the opposite direction down the country lane toward home.

Chauncey noted that Triggerfoot walked slowly, his usual long stride impeded by concentration of thought. The space between his eyebrows was wrinkled like rows of the folded mountain ranges some sixty miles northwest of their home.

Anyone who knew Trig well could tell he was cooking up something in his brainpan, and Chauncey suspected as much.

"Look yonder at that slow walk. He's pondering something, and we'll soon see the results!" Chauncey mumbled as he got on his way.

And, sure enough, it didn't take long, a week, in fact, to the very day.

Another week after that, Chauncey and Trig met once again at Cousin Kildee's store. They were there bright and early, and Cousin Kildee was eager to get more details. The three greeted one another in their usual bluff way.

"Well, Kildee, old man," Triggerfoot said. "How's your symptoms segashuatin today?"

"Fair to middlin', no complaints," Kildee replied in a slow drawl. "And you?"

"I'm about ramstugenous as a ruttin' buck," he said.

"And you, Chaunts?" Trig asked his friend.

"Tolluble," was his reply. They all felt comfortable using community speech, words out of the old time and place. It was almost as good as having what the new set called comfort food. They felt a kind of freedom in violating Webster's rules with the local way. Webster came from a far-away land, after all, where rules pressed their heavy weight on the land. It was conformity and regimentation that ruled in that distant, strange ice-bound land. Stuffy and death dealing, life denying in the extreme.

"Just another part of their culture of death," Chauncey had said to his brother-in-law Clint Blair the other day as they talked about the world and all the laws and rules that seemed to be growing up around them like choking weeds among the crops after a rain.

"Rigid. It's a sure sign rigor mortis is setting in," Clint had answered with a shake of his head. "Seems like Pulliam is more them than us around here. He's got Northern ways."

After a pause, Kildee broached the subject of Pulliam, knowing full well Triggerfoot was involved in the Pulliam affair, an occurrence now getting to be the talk of the town. "Trig, old boy! Old ruttin' buck. Looks like Warn Pulliam's fixing to have a real dilemma this time!"

"I hope he does," was Trig's pithy reply.

Chauncey didn't as yet know much about "the dilemma," as Kildee had phrased it—only that Pulliam wasn't happy at all. Chauncey had visited Pulliam's gas pump this morning, a thing he rarely did, mainly to glean what information he could. When he paid up inside, Pulliam had looked like he could eat somebody alive. Chauncey figured that lemons could have sweetened the look on his putty-coloured face. His lips were drawn thinner and tighter than their usual thin and tight way. As for information, Chauncey didn't get much more than Pulliam's frown. So as Triggerfoot sat in a cool, shadowy corner of the store with his crackers and sardines, Chauncey asked Kildee to fill him in.

What Kildee had been able to piece together himself was this. When Triggerfoot left so bemused two weeks ago, he'd set straight in to town. Next day, he'd been the storytelling entertainer at a birthday party for an eight-year-old cousin there in Clay Bank. The party had been a standard sort of affair—ice cream, birthday cake, party hats, streamers, and bright balloons. That is, it was a standard production, except for Triggerfoot's stories, and his presence there. As Chauncey would often say, "Nothing's taken for granted when old Trig's around. Nothing's standardardised then!"

So Trig had successfully done his part in making the young birthday lad's day complete. He told some wild adventure tales about hunting panthers and swimming rivers for deer, stories Trig knew would just be suited perfectly to eight-year-old minds. When he wanted, he could have a child's free play of imagination and its ability to have uninhibited fun.

Trig had eaten his share of cake and ice cream, but the lad's mother wanted to pay him a little money too, as she discretely put it, to provide him with a little jingle in the pockets to spend about town.

This, he'd refused, but instead had said, "Miss Myrtice, you've got that whole box of coloured balloons there that you didn't use. Must be a thousand left over."

"Yes, Cousin Trig," she replied. "Like everything else now, I couldn't buy just a few. Had to buy a whole big box of the things. Don't know what I'll ever do with a thousand balloons."

"I'd like to have 'em all, Cousin Myrtice, if you please."

This was done and Trig had walked on his way.

Trig knew everybody in town and just where he could get the next item he'd need. He found and borrowed the two little tanks of helium forthwith.

Kildee was in town too, and had given Trig a ride home, with his box of balloons, twin helium tanks, and all. That's how he'd been able to piece together this part of the tale.

So back home at his farmhouse the next day, Trig began to set himself to his task. His farm chores done, he began lettering little cards, three-by-five rectangles of white. This took most of his spare time that day and the next two.

He carefully tied one of these cards to each helium-filled balloon, and let them dance high on their strings in his big farmhouse kitchen till he was through.

"Yessir," Trig said from his corner. "All them bright dancing colours did my heart good, especially knowing what was to come. I had near about a thousand of them pretty darlings: red, pink, yellow, purple, green, white, and blue. Dance, my little pretty ones, I sang. I'll soon give you freedom to fly! And that I did, good as my word, and they did their part too. Fly off they did.

"I let them go all at the same time from the kitchen door. Up they went in all directions, with the wind currents taking them high. My spirits went bounding up with them, soaring up too.

"A red-tail hawk was up there with 'em, riding the currents, gliding, and sailing. He must have rejoiced in what he saw like me, because he kept flying in and about the balloons like he was playing some kind of joyous new hawk's dodge-ball game or threading the line like in an old-fashioned reel. He was dancing on high, and I was playing fiddle for him."

Set free, the balloons cavorted like the hawk and Trig's spirits did, their white cards on the end of their strings blinking in the sun and nodding like the ribbons on a kite's tail. They went all over the county and some into the next, settling down in ploughed fields and stubble fields, on roadsides, in lanes, in pastures where they even surprised cows.

A white balloon came down in a chicken yard where the old hens eyed it, thinking it must be some giant egg. A purple one came to rest on the mirror-smooth grey waters of a farmer's pond. He had to get his johnboat out of his farm shed to retrieve.

A yellow balloon even came to rest on Kildee's own porch there at home. His wife found it—its string caught on the rocker of a chair.

That's how Kildee knew how far they'd flown that day and what Trig had written on the card.

"Yessiree, another stroke of genius, Trig, my lad," Kildee

now complimented him. "You know, Chauncey, old Trig is formidable dangerous, dang me if he ain't. I always want him on my side."

"Then make right sure you stays there," Trig replied.

Kildee paused in his tale. Master teller as he was, he was building suspense, getting the listeners to crave more.

At last, Chauncey couldn't wait any longer. "Well, Kildee, dammit, what was on the card? Don't make us wait till Christmas to find out."

"Simple," Kildee replied, taking his time. "It read in big black letters, block-printed in ink, and covering the whole card:

BRING THIS BALLOON TO WARN PULLIAM'S STORE FOR TEN DOLLARS PRIZE. THIS NOTE IS AS GOOD AS WARN PULLIAM'S WORD.

There was a round of laughter at the store. Chauncey let the words sink in. He was properly impressed by the ingenuity of Trig's scheme, and even more so after knowing the results it achieved.

Indeed, quite a little masterpiece, the note was. It had the potential of meting out country justice, because all that following week, farmers had been coming in to town to Pulliam's, in old pickups and beat-up cars, even in wagons, on foot, and a few coloured folks riding mules. They said they'd found these balloons on their place and were fetching them in to claim their ten-dollar prize.

Pulliam's dilemma was deep and complete. He'd have to

let the cash go—the hardest thing in the world for him—or else he'd lose customers by the score a-plenty, who all had relatives and friends. They'd talk and pass round his refusal to pay, tell everyone the news of it as these country folk did. It was always their way; they didn't need newscast or the New York Times.

Kildee figured that Pulliam had no way out of Triggerfoot's vise. He couldn't afford not to give the ten-dollar reward.

Kildee ran a store too and knew the psychology of business full well. This card looked like it was made up to be a promotional gimmick to get you to come in. Then if you did, and didn't get the promised prize, you'd feel cheated in a big way—betrayed in such a manner to make the customer feel hurt, and perhaps even mad. He'd remember the broken promise for the rest of his life, and Pulliam's word would forever then be known universally to be as much a hoax as the balloon. His every move would be watched closely as being suspect. No more pinkie-finger scale cheating then!

Yes, Pulliam would have to pay, no matter how many balloons came in. Either pay or he might as well close up shop.

"Old Warn has finally got his comeuppance," Kildee declared. "Looks like he's reaped a whirlwind of balloons."

"And richly deserved too," Mr. Lyman agreed. "He's just having to pay back in lump sums a little of what he's stolen from these here same folks for years, a penny and nickel at a time. My wife says that it appears to her that Pulliam's just one of them old-time cheating Yankee pedlars in modern disguise, like them that sold mahogany sawdust for red pepper or nutmegs and pumpkin seeds carved out of wood."

Old Mr. Lyman Eppes had quietly come in the store and heard the end of the tale. He knew Pulliam too, and his ways.

"Yep," he continued. "Pulliam can't win on this one. He's badly outfoxed this time. You're right, Kildee. If those farmers who come in riding so far on mules don't get what they're promised, they'll be peed at Pulliam forever, and tell all their kin. Then if Pulliam gives out the dollars, he'll be forced into being generous, a thing new to him, a heavy cross to bear."

Chauncey was once again mightily impressed by his friend's inventive mind and the essential rightness of his deeds. "That's a funny story," he complimented his friend.

Trig paused awhile and said, "Funny. Yep." He paused again and asked, "Chaunts, you know the opposite of funny?"

"Serious, I reckon," Chauncey replied.

"Got you there," Trig bantered. "It ain't serious, just not funny. That's all."

Right again, Trig's funny was often serious enough, or Pulliam at least would think so this go round. But what really occupied Chauncey's mind even more than marvelling at his friend's cleverness was trying to envision the scene when that first farmer presented the first balloon. He'd like to have been there to see the look in Pulliam's usually cold and expressionless eyes—maybe a look of puzzlement mingled with fear, then turning to panic with the appearance of the second and third, on down to the fiftieth balloon.

"Dang it, if that hadn't been worth good hard money to see," Trig exclaimed.

"Rightly so," old Mr. Lyman agreed.

Chauncey vowed to himself that he'd have to learn the details of how Pulliam took it by asking one of those men who'd taken in a balloon.

What he did find out some days hence was that Pulliam had sent his young overworked and underpaid clerk across town to the local bank to get a banded bundle of a hundred ten-dollar bills. And the breeze must have carried the balloons out yonder quite far, for from all accounts, they were still coming in.

Some weeks later, when all the flurry of this had somewhat settled down and only an occasional balloon was seen and brought in for a claim, Trig had the final comment on the affair when he and Chauncey sat by Trig's fire, there at the big stone hearth in Trig's old farmhouse, sharing the fire's warmth, good conversation, and the mellowness of some of Trig's best scuppernong wine.

"Scales finally always tips out right and true," Trig told his friend.

In answer, the fire popped and the logs settled, nestling down on the hearth.

After a pause, Trig concluded with his slow thoughtful drawl: "A cheatin' finger can unbalance the weighing of things in the great world only for a little while. In the Maker's good time though, the scales balance arrow-straight like a ruler-drawn line and the world sets perfect plumb like with a carpenter's bob."

The logs spewed and the coals glowed a cheerful cherry red.

After another pause, Chauncey picked up Trig's thought. "Yes, in the Kingdom of Thingdom, He measures with that same plumb-bob and when that Kingdom is lacking, like Isaiah says, it's just a matter of time till the judgement falls."

"And the golden towers all come tumbling down on Babylon worse than London bridge," Trig added with a serious look at the glowing coals.

Chauncey drowsily nodded his head in agreement. Then the two relished the silence as Chauncey considered the rightness of his friend's observation about scales being set straight—correct at least in a world where there still existed men like his friend.

V

A Grave Adventure

Some weeks after the Warn Pulliam affair had settled down, Triggerfoot was seated comfortably on his favourite cane-bottomed chair, his legs spread wide and his hands on his knees so that he looked like a sturdy pyramid. The chair was an old one made and stained indigo blue by a friend who'd died many years ago—back when Trig was in his twenties. The dead friend's children had given Trig the old fellow's drawing knife, froe, and several other farm tools, which he accepted with thanks. But Trig dropped his usual manners in matters like this and downright asked for the chair.

"You mind if I have Mister Pink's old blue chair?" he'd asked.

"Of course," the daughter replied and let him bring it home to his farmhouse that very day he asked.

It had sat in the same place by Trig's hearth from that time on, for over a quarter of a century now. It was in the place of honour by his fire, and there were only a few in the world to whom he'd offer the seat. He himself usually sat where he could see, rather than be in it. Maybe deep down, he felt he was saving the chair for the friend who'd used it in life. Trig sometimes felt that perhaps he did sit there too, only unseen by the living's limited eyes.

Fifty years of hard use would have caused the chair bottom to go; but careful as Trig was with it, he'd been required to replace only one hickory strip or two. These he cut with the friend's own drawing knife from a tree in Trig's woods. His friend had taught him the craft. In so many ways, Trig's hands repeated the rhythm of his friend's.

"Old Mister Pink," Trig said aloud to the fireplace flames.

That Trig was seated in the chair today betokened something special. Sitting with him was Chauncey, his best living friend, and who'd taken a seat in Trig's overstuffed armchair.

They'd both been helping several folks from out of town—one a lady from far off Alabama—in finding an old family burying plot. There lay buried the lady's great-great-great-grandsire, before that grandsire's son, her great-great-grandfather, had moved westward in the time of "Go west young man."

The barns and deserted farmhouses all over this area of upcountry Carolina in those far-off days had scrawled on them with charcoal or chalk or painted hurriedly in whitewash in big letters on weathering wood **G.T.T.** No one needed telling that the initials meant **GONE TO TEXAS**—only her ancestor hadn't got farther than Alabama.

"Now, it's something," Trig told Chauncey. "To come five hundred miles to look for a plot of ground you've never seen and don't rightly even know is there. That's faith and devotion. I'm just glad we found that sunken piece of earth with the battered old fieldstone. It's a wonder we could with the place covered up so in such a tangle of blackberry briars. Nearly tore my pants legs off getting through."

"And wasn't she excited," Chauncey recalled. "She almost dropped the topo map. She whipped out that digital camera from her tote bag so fast I didn't even see, and must have made a dozen photos from every angle she could."

"Good thing we'd thought to bring a hoe so we could chop out the honeysuckle and briars," said Trig. "Or she wouldn't have been able to photograph a thing, fancy camera or no."

"Said she'd send us some copies e-mail, till I told her I didn't have a computer," Chauncey remembered he'd said.

Usually, this would have started one or both of the men on a discussion of how the world was rushing headlong to hell with its machines, how the machine worship was not short of idolatry these days and would likely result in no good end, how all the expensive up-to-date equipment in the world would have been worthless on their trip without the humble old hoe. Trig often wondered what catastrophe the future would bring because of man's willfulness and lack of proper restraint in the things that they ought to be restrained in. But today Trig was looking backward, not ahead.

He declared in serious tone, "Now, it's fine to hunt up your dead. That's a kind of honouring of them that I expect they'd appreciate. But I'll bet the way that we got there may have made them same old-timers laugh."

"Yep," agreed Chauncey. "I thought when that fallen tree was across the path and the so-called unstoppable all-terrain vehicle couldn't get over it, that the party's confidence was shaken to the core. Did you see how that man from Greenville's jaw dropped?"

"Weren't their faces pitiful though," Trig recalled.

"Yeah, they looked back and forth at each other like the world had come to an end. *Pitiful*'s not the word for it. If it hadn't been for us, they'd never got past that place in the road. Several good strong backs, arms, and legs can still solve problems an all-terrain vehicle can't start to comprehend. There's some terrain I reckon the car makers ain't been."

"Right as rain," Trig agreed. "Problem with machines like that is that they're made by men who think the world has been planned and constructed by men, and just for men. They can usually do fine enough on a man-made road, but don't let a God-made tree fall over their neat man-made plan."

"Most machines are like that. They're good for their little specialty and just for doing that one thing or two that they're made to do. But don't let them get out of that tiny place. The gadget made to do one thing is as worthless as counterfeit bills when put to another task."

"Yep, that is, if it's working, and ain't broke, which it usually is, and with no one who knows how to fix it," Trig put in.

"But who could guess we'd have a great washed-out fifteen-foot-deep gulley to cross just around the road's next bend," Trig remembered. "Out of the vehicles again, and this time we had to leave them behind. The lady bore up well under the rough two-mile walk, better than the city men. I'll sure give her that. And the briars tearing her fancy pants and jacket too."

"Yes, she's a trooper. These genealogist women are a new kind of general, commanding forced marches of men," Chauncey declared.

"I thought that time when she tripped on a limb and sprawled on all fours, that'd be the end, but up she got, put her crushed hat back on, adjusted her torn jacket, and we were at it again." Trig paused as he remembered the scene.

"Yep, I had to admire her. A real trooper."

"And not bad looking either. Chaunts, I saw you looking at them long legs. Had plenty chance in that sprawl." Trig adjusted himself in the chair. "But if they'd just asked me from the start, I'd of saved them lots of grief and time. The man from Greenville went everywhere around here trying to borrow or rent some kind of off-road vehicle. When he finally got a couple, he thought his problems were solved. But he soon found out his trials had just begun. Lucky we got his borrowed things out alive and in one piece—them and us with them too."

"What would you have done?" Chauncey was curious to know.

"Well, there's a natural easy solution to their all-terrain problem," Triggerfoot answered without pause. "They could just have used a couple of mules. Mules are surefooted and steady, easy to ride. Even if them city folks had never been near one, would have taken only a minute to learn."

"True," Chauncey replied. "And you've got Flag Jr. and

Fodder-eater, and I've got old Jake and Dove. They could have had them for the easy asking."

"I wouldn't ever take anything but Fodder with me on any kind of hunt, squirrel, turkey, or deer," Trig declared. "Because he's quiet, not raising racket and turmoil like these machines, scaring everything to cover that you're trying to find. And he can go anywhere. Mules don't have to stay on paths and roads."

He paused awhile, then continued, "You've seen all those men around lately—from way-off Atlanta, I think they said—with cell phones and walkie-talkies and a convoy of fast jeeps, coming over here to deer hunt? Last week they were tearing through the woods making so much racket no deer would have shown its scut for ten miles around.

"Well, and then here comes an ambulance a little later with its flashing red lights and blaring horns. Seems one of the fellows sitting up high in the back of a jeep had run under a low cedar limb and got clotheslined. Scraped him right off the vehicle and near broke his neck. His rifle fell with him too, and it fired off into the woods, clipping branches as it went. The cedar caught another one of the riders flat in the face and broke his nose. Blood spurting everywhere. He was gouged and so covered with blood you couldn't tell what there was left on his face. The third one lost an eye. They say the limb plumb scraped off his nose. Had to helicopter him to Columbia. Serious stuff this—just for a lark. Wonder is there wasn't somebody killed."

"I heard about that too," Chauncey added. "And I heard

the same ambulance was needed with another such city crew the very next week. Seems this crowd from Charlotte was more after speed in their jeep than deer. The driver lurched into high gear with his powerful engine, and the man sitting perched on the back lost his balance and fell off. He hit the ground hard and dislocated his shoulder. The rifle fell with him and discharged. Lucky, it only shot out the tire of the vehicle, but besides his shoulder, he also broke his leg in a compound fracture—bone sticking out and all. And another ambulance screaming through the land. But it's their damn-fool necks, and if they want to break them, it's their business, I reckon. Just so they leave me alone."

"What a heap of trouble money can bring," Triggerfoot said solemnly. "Especially in the hands of them that don't have nothing better to do. 'More dollars than sense,' Pa always said."

"Trig, if you had that kind of money just one of these four wheelers or dirt bikes cost, you could make some real improvements around here."

"Well, I don't reckon I ever will," Trig answered his friend. "And I don't care none if I don't. I'm just glad that Alabama lady found her great-great-great-grandpappy's stone."

"Yep. She was pleased as she could be. I could see it in her eyes. It was mission accomplished. The general won her war."

"It was more like she won the skirmish," corrected Trig. "She was following through and was going to put up a marker for the grave, giving proper dates and all. But doing this turned out to be the real battle, a worse one than finding the place."

Trig coloured a little as he spoke. "Since the grave had the misfortune to be on National Forest Land, they'd not give permission, and she had to get a lawyer and go to court and sue. She finally won, but the decision said she wasn't allowed to use but thirty-five words. She was hot, believe me, and I don't blame her at all. She got her revenge though because she put on the backside of the granite marker in carved out words that the details on the rock are sketchy because the regulations allowed her only thirty-five words. I bet that burned some official arse."

"Does sound like a worse ordeal," Chauncey agreed. "And on land the government bought for a dollar an acre back in the hard depression times, when folks couldn't do any better and weren't able to hold on. Her family's land! Adding insult to injury. She said it was worse than Cromwell's land grab in Ireland, where the man whose grave she was marking had been forced to leave for sassing his English landlord on land that he'd once owned. Wonder is he wasn't hanged, she said."

The two men paused for a moment.

"Same old evil story," Chauncey declared. "Folks in power beating up on folks just wanting to be left alone to live in peace on God's good land."

"I believe she's doing some sort of book on her kin." Trig said. With this comment, he passed Chauncey his jug.

"Wonder why mules are out of favour these days, Chaunts, old friend. Who'd not rather be able to talk to the thing that's not doing what you want it to do and have it to hear you fuss and cuss. If you're going to have something that frustrates you, at least let it be something you can kick and it know."

Chauncey agreed.

After a pause to savour and do justice to Trig's art of the jug, his "farming in the woods," as he called his whiskey-making routine, Trig pulled out a little black plastic rectangle from the hip pocket of his jeans.

It was one of the Atlanta men's walkie-talkies, with its highly polished dials shining bright as when purchased from its fancy Dunwoody electronics store.

"When I went over to Mr. Lyman's to see the scene of the crime where the ambulance had stormed in, I found the ground all tore up, even some blood. This thing was lying right there face up on a little pile of broken-up twigs."

"No way to get it to the men, I reckon." Trig turned the plastic rectangle in his hand. "And so what good is one walkie-talkie to them or to me? It sure does take two. I carry it around, thinking I'll see one of the men."

After another thoughtful pause, he continued, "Somehow, I reckon that about sums up their scene. They're navigating the world with half a walkie-talkie. Trig's got the missing half, but they'll never ask, not thinking of me. And Trig don't need theirs because he usually knows well enough where he is. But they're lost here without his half, if you see what I mean."

"Reckon I do, Trig. Reckon I do. And I don't expect they'll be coming back this way to claim it, after all that's happened to them here. They've probably had enough adventure to last them awhile. We'll probably never see them again."

This time when the jug was passed, Chauncey declined. He'd begun to feel the effects of his several chugs and knew when the enough mark was achieved.

Instead of taking a drink, he commented on Trig's cheery fire, made from wood cut with his own axe from ancestral woods. "You know, Trig, civilisation took a great tumble when the open fireplace was given up for the furnace and electric heat."

"And so did hillsides and mountaintops blown away to get coal to run electric plants, and free running rivers and streams dammed up to turn turbine machines."

Both fell silent at that, in a moment of quiet to memorialise the loss of hills, mountaintops, and free flowing streams. Chauncey looked at the dancing flames. Their fire's warmth fell on his skin and imparted peace of mind.

"Better to watch this show together," Chauncey said after awhile. "Than an infernal TV screen. You can't talk when you do. If you did, you'd be accounted rude."

"A crazy world," Trig replied.

After a season of silence interspersed with a few observations upon this and that and news of the community, Chauncey said that he'd better get on his way home. Still, he kept his seat and didn't venture to move.

Trig shifted his weight, and without rising, put the black plastic rectangle on the mantelshelf above him. There it sat in the half-light next to a battered ancient brass candlestick and a gilt-framed image of his ma and pa. The picture shared space with a cone-shaped punched-tin lantern that Trig's grandpa said had served his own great-grandpa, Golding Tinsley, lighting his way in camp against the British at Musgrove's Mill, King's Mountain, and the Battle of Hannah's Cowpens a piece up the road. Over the lantern was a battered sword, used by Trig's great-granddaddy Tinsley in 1861. It hung horizontal on its frayed gold cord. The firelight glinted off its blade.

"Got to get on home," Chauncey said again, but both still looked at the fire for a spell as if hypnotised.

Trig broke the silence this time. "What's your hurry, Chaunts? Sitting's cheaper than riding, or walking too. All you need is this here free honest chair."

"No walkie-talkie needed between us either," Chauncey answered, meeting Trig's eye. "We can talk face to face. And you've usually got something worth the hearing to say. Guess I just *will* sit a few minutes more. What other wisdom have you got for me today?"

"None that I know of right off," answered Trig. He took the question seriously. Chauncey could tell that his tribute was properly appreciated. There was quiet again.

As Chauncey walked to his truck through Trig's neatly ploughed late-winter fields, he noticed a sign on a cedar post. *PRIVATE* it read. Not that Trig was unfriendly, but he didn't want folks with no business there nosing around.

Chauncey had to chuckle when he saw another Trig had just put up. *NO TRESPASSING. SURVIVORS WILL BE PROSERCUTED.* This was lettered in red, the paint in places running down.

Chauncey went on his way. Things were coming together for him at last, and he was in good spirits, such good spirits that he could hum a little song.

The full moon was rising straight ahead. It looked heavy with promise. Its light tinged the world silver and made long shadows to the right and left of him as he drove.

Down the road a piece, a doe with her fawn stood at the road's gravel edge. He slowed, but the two didn't move. He saw the bright spots of the little one. They followed him with their eyes. Farther on, a possum scuttled quickly across the pavement. The truck lights made the strange eyes in its skull-shaped head shine an eerie green. It turned its head to look at him as it ran. At the entrance to his lane stood a shaggy bobcat as solemn sentinel. It didn't move from its perch on the high bank of the old roadbed cut deep in wagon and carriage days. He was so close to the animal that he could see the hairy points of its ears in the truck's beams. The cat watched him as he made the turn and then dissolved into the dark woods.

Chauncey enjoyed the drive home. He knew an efficient short cut but had driven the long way instead.

At the kitchen table, he sat with a sheet of paper and dipped his pen. Trig's talk of mules and how they'd gotten out of fashion occasioned some lines. "Prescience," he wrote the title. Then the poem took form.

I wonder
If mules
Suspected

When they saw
Wagon wheels
Painted red
And white
And green
And used
At
Subdivisions'
Gates.

He'd just seen a new pair of them erected on an elaborate brick and granite base at the entrance to Plantation Estates on the outskirts of Clay Bank town.

He looked at the cleanly lined words on the bright page. Like short furroughs themselves, he thought. *Verse*, to turn, the turn of the plough at the row's end. He mused on the ancients and how everything genuine today went back to the cultivation of the soil. Origins. And how few people knew how little they considered the foundations of their day. *Boustrophedon* he said aloud, relishing the sound. *Turning like an ox when ploughing.* How close the ancient poets were to the land, and how removed our time.

It was getting late, too late to start a fire, so he placed his sheet on the little stack building in his reading alcove. A new kind of hayrick, he thought, as he turned out the light, and sought the comfort of quilts.

VI
School

~⟋∾⟍~

On the matter of riding and walking, both Trig and Chauncey knew a thing or two. Chauncey tried to walk wherever and whenever he could. Trig made sure of that by not having a truck or car. Folks might take him places when they were going the same way, but this didn't happen too often, except with Chauncey, who made certain Trig had transportation when the necessity came along.

This rainy March day, Chauncey's brother-in-law Clint was at Kildee's store. All chores done, Chauncey had given Trig a ride there, and the talk was lively enough around the potbellied stove.

Clint had now successfully graduated from vet school and was beginning to get him some work around that part of the world. Because of the rain, there wasn't much for him to do today, or, in fact, for Trig or Chauncey either.

So the three settled in to their usual easy conversational give and take. Attard Connelly, a neighbour down the road, sat in a fourth rocker around the stove. Kildee's chair, which he'd now and then occupy during the lulls in his work, made part of the circle.

Today Trig was especially interested in getting Clint to tell about that university world from which he'd just come.

Chauncey had taken Trig over there to Clint's school for an afternoon three years ago. On that visit, Chauncey was dropping off some things from home that Clint needed and would use the occasion for them to visit a few hours.

It was a fine May day. The trees on campus were greening up once again and the youthful faces of the coeds looked to Trig like flowers in bloom. They met Clint at school, and the three talked as they walked across campus to town for a bite to eat—or tried to talk, that is.

There was a man on a high-powered riding lawn mower over which not a syllable could be heard. Clint got in a few words; then they met a man in goggles with a fancy leaf blower that drowned out everything Clint said. Chauncey was getting out of patience.

They walked on. Trig got in a few words and there was the riding mower again. It had circled back around in its cutting routine. It had to pause a few seconds for the leaf blower man to get by. Then round and round it went, getting dizzying fast.

"If this don't beat all," Chauncey said.

Clint was trying to tell them some of the things he'd been into of late, but neither Chauncey nor Trig could do more than guess at his narration's drift. They could tell by Clint's animated expressions and gestures that the story was something they'd like to hear.

Clint got in a whole sentence this time, and then to add insult to injury, there was another goggled man with another gas-powered machine—a five-foot-tall handheld sidewalk edger. It had its own particular unhappy grumble and roar. It vied with the sound of a motorised hedge trimmer.

"If this just doesn't tear it! A place that's supposed to be a haven for thought and ideas and it's so noisy with machines you can't even hear yourself think, much less talk." Chauncey was really out of patience now.

They had passed through the school's iron arch into the life of the town. Now the noise of trucks and cars greeted them. Traffic was bumper to bumper, or like Trig phrased it, "nose to tail like sniffing dogs." The distant sound of an ambulance came to their ears. The gears of a bus screeched to a halt.

"Whew!" said Trig. "Smell that gasoline! And I used to think mule farts was bad."

"The smell of money burning," Clint volunteered.

They settled into Clint's favourite little diner on Broad Street. It wasn't a chain and had been there for over fifty years, the oldest one downtown, and the only one still locally owned. Once Clint found it, he became a regular, when he had to eat out, that is, for he'd learned to cook as a lad watching and helping his sister Hoyalene after their mother had died. Here he could get a real dinner, not lunch. Lunch he defined as some pitiful something you could hold in your hand and eat on the run. Clint, like the people back home, still used the words "dinner" and "supper" to describe meals.

"From Broad River to Broad Street, Clint," Trig observed. "What a long way you've come." "Well, at least it's not Broadway," he said.

They visited there in the booth over glasses of tea and plates of fried chicken, almost as good as at home. "This cornbread is good!" Trig declared. Clint said that the restaurant owner's father came in every morning at five to make it and the biscuits.

The waitress was efficient in her casual-seeming way. She hid her busyness with grace like the ladies they knew back home.

Trig took note and was impressed.

"Glad to get out of that noise," Clint declared. "Don't know how I'm going to take it for two more years."

So now, on this March afternoon, Trig was thinking back to his visiting Clint that one time in the university town. He brought up the subject to Mr. Connelly and the two who'd shared the experience with him.

The rain now beat down heavy on the store's old roof.

"Good for the corn," Chauncey observed.

"And all growing things outen the earth," Trig added.

Chauncey could detect reverence in his friend's tone.

"Lucky I got all my ploughing done," Mr. Connelly said. "Thanks to y'all boys."

Clint and Chauncey had helped him, figuring what the weather had in store.

With his usual skilled narrative so full of the concreteness of the experience, Trig took them back to that day in the diner. There at the table Trig had taken up the subject of the men with mowers, leaf blowers, hedge trimmers, and sidewalk edgers. Trig had asked, half seriously, "Wonder if their arms and legs won't just wither away? You know they say if you don't use something for long enough time you and your people to come will have those things just bred out of the creature for all time."

"That's right," Clint had answered. "In vet and med classes we're learning about such things. People's final vertebra at the end of the spine was once the beginning of a tail. When we quit hanging in trees, the prof says, the tail dried up."

"Vestigial's the word," Chauncey had added.

Trig was ready to make a choice comment about one thing he'd not used in a long time and prayed it wouldn't fall off, but the waitress came with more tea.

She was friendly and took time to talk. They kept her busy bringing them refills of tea. It was May but already hot as summer, and the tea glasses sweated and ran onto the paper napkins under them.

Trig had been dressed in his best clothes but hadn't bought anything but flannel shirts and blue jeans for so long he was a little bedraggled looking compared to his two friends. This hadn't phased him a jot, however, and his friends had taken no real notice of it either. He'd gotten only a few stares from passersby, for in truth, with youngsters sporting purple hair, snake and lizard tattoos, and about every body part you could see pierced with rings, the locals had gotten use to about anything. One guy around town even wore a long dress.

"Yep. I remember that day at Clint's college very well," Trig declared. "One of the few times I've ever been away from here. It's a long way to walk over there, so I don't reckon I'll ever get back or want to. Got my diploma from there in one day. Soaked up about all I needed from that place and all it cost was dinner, and worth every penny I paid."

"You got out cheap," Chauncey observed.

"Nope. I don't crave a return."

"Won't miss much either," Clint declared. "Except noise, babbling, and mouth sounds. Felt most of the time all the talking was shapes to fill a lack. That's all."

Clint was able to answer one of Trig's questions as to what he'd learned in that strange sanctuary of contemplation where you couldn't hear yourself think.

"More than leaf-blower noise. There's more and deeper static around that place than with machines. In one class, I learned a fact I've remembered ever since that day. I was taking an ag course, vet school allied. We were talking about walking in the routine of farm work and reading the stats done by a big research project out of, I believe, the Department of Health and Exercise at the University of Tennessee.

"The researchers rigged up men and women with pedometers to measure the number of steps folks take each day. They put these meters on both the traditional Amish and a cross section of just your regular sort of women and men. They came up with 18,400 steps per average Amish man, 14,500 for the average Amish wife. The average non-Amish man took three to five thousand a day."

"I'm not surprised," Chauncey declared. "Even the grounds crew at such places just ride and the teachers and students sit in classrooms or at desks most of the day. They drive or ride buses from class to class."

Clint remembered he'd walked to his apartment that day after class and counted his steps. Only a thousand steps home, and round trip, he'd not even measured more than two thousand, far short of the 18,000 for the Amish man. The rest of the day was just sitting around. It was then that he knew it was time to get out of that world as soon as he could before his legs withered away.

"The lesson to be learned from the stats that day in class was that as a farmer you couldn't afford not to buy and use machines. The Amish way was romantic but not practical. It didn't serve today's agri-industry reality. But I got a clean different lesson. The moral of the story for me was maybe the walkers had the better way."

"Bet that sure wasn't intended in a class that pushes an industrial world that cranks out machines and worships them with their backsides every minute of the day," declared Chauncey.

"No wonder the country's so bad overweight," Mr. Connelly observed. "We've got everything done by machine. As our lifestyles get fatter and larger, our heinies do too."

There was a pause. "Noisy damn machines," Chauncey grumbled. He wondered how many steps he'd take on average each day. Like his two friends, he was trim and wiry from work, though Clint had softened a little, especially around the middle, with his six years at school.

There was another pause. Chauncey broke the silence. "And then there's Proctor and Gamble," he said. "Making everything easier for us, wives and all. The ads say, 'You don't have to scrub. Just spray and wash it away. Effortless. No elbow grease.' Seems the whole culture's aim is to avoid using limbs. Physical work, I reckon, has become the most shameful thing, the only real evil, to be avoided before sin."

"For most folks, it is *the* sin," Mr. Connelly agreed.

"And one of the worst things about being poor," Clint added, "Is that you don't have the bucks to buy all those things that save you the pains of using your limbs."

"You're sure right, Attard. It's work and sweat that's the sin," Trig added. "'Bout the only sin. After being poor, that is."

The three continued to reminisce about that day at the restaurant in Clint Blair's world. Clint recalled that another reason he'd liked the diner was that its owner tried whenever possible to use vegetables and meats raised as nearby as they could get them. Chauncey said he was able to tell from the taste. And now Clint could volunteer another statistic he'd learned from that class at school. He loved statistics, this prof did. Made him sound more like a scientist, those most respected of men in the college world.

"My prof said that the average food travels 1,600 miles before we eat. Tomato varieties are developed for long keeping and picked green. Then sometimes shipped for three thousand miles."

"Hard to believe," Trig had answered. "So, if I was to *buy* a tomato sammich, it would be better travelled than me.

And smarter and more cultured too because it's seen more of the world."

"And the tomatoes would taste like cardboard," Clint replied. "As all of us know, if you've never eaten one that's homegrown, you've never eaten one. What a mess this whole growing-our-food has become. Too scientific. Too automated. Too assembly lined. Too many wheels on too many machines. And what passes for education seems to follow the model too, with those in charge like CEOs."

There was a long pause.

"If I was to look a fast-food hamburger full in the face, I'd get an inferiority complex," Trig said. "I'll never track as many miles as it's come, and it dead, and me still alive, and never likely to leave home."

"You ain't missing much," Mr. Connelly said. "The wheel's a great thing, but you can take anything to the extreme. I drove a big rig for seven years when our farm hit a tight, and when me and my wife got things straightened out and out of debt, we prayed I'd never have to do that again. Being on four wheels is bad enough, but just think about eighteen."

"Well, Clint, from what you say, seems like they're turning out a lot of office drones, technicians, and wage slaves," Trig volunteered. "Maybe your university ought to teach the danger of machines instead of worshiping them."

"That ain't likely to happen, Trig. They're just like the culture that produces the school—the machine culture full of parking lots and shrines to the car," Chauncey said. "How else would you expect the school to be? It's just a reflection of what moves the world. After all, 'The Age demanded . . .'"

And Clint finished him, "'. . . an image of its accelerated grimace,'" quoting a line of poetry from Chauncey's old standby *Mauberley.*

Chauncey nodded approvingly at Clint and continued: "But, yes, you'd hope they'd be smarter and on top of things. They're supposed to be. Leastways, that's what we think we pay them to be."

"I expect it's big industry and government that pays as much as us," added Mr. Connelly. "And that's what them big boys want. As for us, our money don't talk because it don't have a voice, since they don't ask us. Take us for granted, I reckon, and get away with PR and scam."

"Too much like a tech school and no long view," Clint declared. "A tech school in the Parking Lot Nation."

Clint's comment surprised Chauncey a little, and he was pleased to the tip of his toes. *Becoming more and more like a son than many sons*, he thought.

There at the diner that day Clint had told them, "The other day, the local papers did a PR job for the school, which is the town's top-paying biggest 'industry,' as they say. Biggest payroll, in the millions every month. The paper pictured a top university man sitting smiling a broad smile in the cockpit of a Raptor bomber aircraft. Smiling so pleased, with a thumbs-up gesture with his right hand, and me so ashamed. Can you believe it! But seems all this PR had to do with getting government grants and conforming the university's programs to meet the Raptor manufacturer's employment needs. It's all about money, you see. Big business as usual around here. From the stadium to the classroom."

"Just like in most criminal cases, follow the money," Trig said.

They remembered how Chauncey had been stunned to silence for a while. Then he'd declared, "So I reckon now the school's main mission is to kill. *Raptor.* That's not a very nice word when the prey is men. It falls way outside what you ought to expect of schools. Just the opposite, by rights, of what they should be. But things are backwards nowadays. Right's wrong and wrong's right. Everything's twisted around. Pretty's ugly and ugly's pretty. Good's bad and bad's good. Everything's out of kilter and off key. The world lives by a lie, and the lie gets celebrated as truth. I just read what Pope John Paul called this kind of world. A culture of death, he said."

"Well, he sounds right to me," Trig had declared. "The Good Book says that the person who loves truth loves God, and those who love God love life."

"Well, this twisted world loves and lives a lie," Chauncey continued. "Seems to me it's about come to love death."

Trig agreed.

Clint added, "Like Mr. Lyman says so often, 'These is evil times.'"

"And seems they're getting worse, not better," Chauncey reflected after a pause, putting his empty tea glass down.

With the four big glasses of tea he'd drunk, Trig had

begun to look around the restaurant for a restroom.

"Gents is this way," the waitress had pointed, intuiting his need, and Trig went in search.

While Trig was gone, Chauncey had kept on sharing the fond news of home. Clint wanted to know each detail of what, where, when, why, and whom, especially about a young lady by the name of Ida Jessine Alston. Knowing through the grapevine that Chauncey was about to go over to see Clint, she'd sent him the request to say hello. Chauncey said he knew right then that Clint was aching to get back home as soon as he could and that the home turf was more dear to him than the pampered and machine-manicured sod they'd just trodden upon.

"Ida seems to be getting prettier every time I see her," Chauncey said.

Clint was about to say something, but Trig had come back from the bathroom. They'd paid their bills and had driven Clint home. Trig and Chauncey had then made the four hours back to Clay Bank and their farms. Yes, they remembered well that day three years ago and how much they'd enjoyed seeing Clint and sitting down with their heads together and their feet under the same table for a meal, even in a foreign land.

The rain had slacked now on the store's tin, and Chauncey went out back to take him a good whiz. When he came back in, Trig and Clint took their turns.

"Trig, you want to know what else I learned another day at school?" Clint picked up the thread. "More statistics and statistics that mattered to me then and now." He laughed. "It's about taking a pee. Taking one out back just now reminded me. This was in a water resources seminar. If I can remember straight, the stats went that if a quarter of the men in the U.S. saved one flush a day by whizzing outside, we'd save more than four billion cubic feet of chemical-treated water a year, and at three whizzes a day, twelve billion cubic feet."

"Well, I do my part. I'm a native streamer complete," said Trig. "And with more than three flushes a day. So does Chauncey here."

Clint remembered more of that day at his desk in the classroom, "Yes, and the stats were rolling on. I didn't know whether to laugh or look impressed. At 2.5 gallons a flush, the professor declared, urinating outside once a day would save nearly a thousand gallons per year, and three times a day, three thousand gallons a year. Multiply that by a million men and the figure is three billion gallons saved a year."

"And all that chlorine and fluorine," Chauncey said. "Chemical companies would hate that. Probably put some of them out of business, for sure, and stop them from killing more rivers at the same time."

Clint remembered that a classmate had raised his hand and volunteered that a friend of his had relieved himself behind a bush on College Street after drinking a pitcher of beer at a student nightspot down town and got arrested and fined a fat fine. "Public Indecency" was the charge, and it stuck. The professor had ignored the comment as if he hadn't heard.

Mr. Lyman had now joined them in the circle around the stove. He warmed his hands and drew up a rocker. "But better than saving water and chemicals and all that," he declared. "It marks your territory."

"And helps to keep away deer," added Kildee.

"So, you mean that it's more than knocking off leaves from bushes in the fall, drawing pictures or writing your name in the snow, or outening campfires at hunt camps at the end of the day?" Mr. Lyman asked, but was really not seeking an answer. "All this hubbub about not aiming at a hole," he continued. "As I've said before, we lives in mixed up times. Today, we cook outside and crap inside. Just backwards, I say. Don't need no statistics for that to show. And bassackwards in more than one way. Dern if it ain't a crazy world!" Mr. Lyman didn't know it, but his words were in perfect line and harmony with what his friends had just been saying.

As the oldest one, it was fitting he had the last say. His words left their echo in the walls. That's the way the younger men wanted it, desired it to be, in the natural order of things. One day, in time, God willing, they'd have their turn. And they weren't rushing the day. As they knew, responsibility came with that turf. There was no real generation gap in their world. Chauncey figured that was for the alienated, getting-and-spending, pushing-and-shoving, fragmented world of strife, of the struggle on the darkling plain of ignorant armies clashing by night, of the hyped struggle of class and gender and race, even age—signs of the Raptor's selfish, I-centred culture of death. Deracination complete. Chauncey thought on, "Yes, for the moneyed, self-destroying Me-generation writ large—and most certainly not the concern of community that stood at the solid base of rooted identity, and wisdom, of family, hearth, and a well-loved place." Chauncey saw these last things as the sum total of their own communal culture of life, of continuities, wholeness, and health, and their *live and let live* philosophy—Kildee's own motto. He had no illusion about how the world felt about their way. It thought them backward and unprogressive, or at best beneath their regard; but he had an ally in one of his favourite poets. "To be sane in a mad time," he'd proclaimed, "Is bad for the brain." Darn right he was out of step with the world, and he took much comfort in that. He also thought of Yeats and interpreted his rough, rude beast of the new order as science and socialism— the masters of the century, the new God of the land. He knew Yeats well enough to figure that's what he'd meant by the creature slouching toward Bethlehem to be born.

And as for the industrial devourer that gorged itself on red clay and women and men too, he had only a hatred that went far deeper than disdain.

"You know folks," Trig broke the silence around the glowing stove. "Old Missus Livingston down the road from me just had her own run-in with a machine. Her grown son Vernon, who still lives with her at home, was combining silage and fell off the combine. It bruised him up but didn't hurt him all that bad. Nothing broke, nothing really injured but his dignity. Got jabbed by stubble in his arm and cheek.

"Old Parson Blum come over to see her, she told me, and asked her how Vernon was. Before she thought real good, she told him that Vernon wasn't doing all that well because yesterday he'd fallen off his concubine. Parson Blum looked a little puzzled for awhile, then had to laugh out loud. 'I'm glad you're reading your Scripture, Missus Livingston,' is all that he said. And as for concubines and combines, the falls from grace is near about the same, only from the combine it's a much longer fall and hurts a lot more when you hits the ground.'"

The fellowship of the stove had to agree.

Even from inside, they could tell the weather was clearing now. Through the store's sooty windows, the sky showed a cold electric blue. The afternoon was passing apace, and there were the evening chores to be done. After saying they had to be going home the obligatory three or four times, the men finally took their leave. Clint went his way, and Chauncey, in Blue Bessie, chugged Trig on back home with three statistical lessons learned. He related them in his mind. Chauncey declared it was good that all those government grants and university seminars came together to put the explanation of figures to the important points of their lives, which they out of common sense already knew—pointers like peeing outside. And even Trig exercised uncharacteristic restraint in resisting the temptation to make a pun out of *pointers*.

VII
The Midnight Oil

~•~

A few weeks later, Chauncey was seated in his comfortable big armchair in his reading alcove. Spring was now fully in the air; and this clear, bright day had been a busy one. Still, he'd saved a precious hour to pick up his lessons.

"Lessons at my age," he muttered as his fingers smoothed the frays on the worn chintz of the chair's arms.

It was a flowered print of gardenias and yellow jessamine vines picked out by Hoyalene the first month of their marriage. He distinctly remembered the day. Although worn, the cloth had too many memories to replace. He'd just use it the way it was, maybe lay pieces of cotton cloth over the frays.

The lesson was Latin. He was teaching himself laboriously. Now self-graduated to the third-year grammar after more years than three, Chauncey felt some satisfied. The old dog was learning new tricks. He especially wanted to be able to read some of Hesiod, some of the *Eclogues* and *Georgics*, and Marcus Cato. This was his goal, and he'd been successful enough in his studies to begin his Vergil with the help of a literal translation he'd picked up at a used bookstore.

When he'd visited Clint at school in the Kingdom of Thingdom, as the two called it, he'd always stopped by the used bookstore. That was the best place in town, far as he was concerned, a real place of learning, with possibilities unchecked. From there, he'd built up a nice tidy little library of those Latin and Greek texts that interested him.

This afternoon, he was studying the root meaning of the word *agriculture*, appropriately, for it was a word his daily work and way of life revolved around.

"*Ager, agri,*" he pronounced aloud. The word for a ploughed field.

"*Ager,*" he repeated. "Tilled rows." He looked up for a moment and then out the window at old bronze stubble fields with the sunlight playing on them in and out of puffy fast moving clouds, and waiting for the plough.

Its diametric opposite, to the Latin mind, oddly enough, *campus.*

"*Campus,*" Chauncey said slowly, giving it the Latin inflection, last syllable stressed. Chauncey found this opposition interesting. His mind held the word and its meaning, fingering it like an orange, unpeeling the lobed sections of the fruit.

"An unploughed field," its meaning read. He was about to ponder the deeper suggestions of that when the loud scrapes of shoe soles on the bottom step roused him from thought. Somebody was cleaning the clay from his feet.

Then the long, quick stride across the boards of the floor beat like a muffled drum, and he had no doubt who was soon at the door.

"Triggerfoot," he said out loud with pleasure and smiled.

Indeed, there was his tall silhouette against the sun.

Trig knocked merrily at the same time he opened the screen door and gave out a call.

"Chauncey, hide the woman! If you're nekkid, put on some clothes."

Matter of fact, Chauncey half was. He'd had his bath after working up a sweat this day and was in his armchair in T-shirt and boxers.

As he called to Trig to come on in, he pulled on his old khaki cutoffs and put on his camo shirt.

"Did you walk all the way up here from home?" he asked his friend. Chauncey hadn't heard a truck or car.

"Nope. Spurgeon had come to buy Blossom's new calf and asked if I wanted a ride anywhere on his way back home. He dropped me off at the gate down the way once we saw Blue Bessie in the yard. We figured you'd give me a ride to my house, or if not, I could hoof it on back. Done that before many a time. I love this time of the year. Plenty of stars."

"Yep. You can still walk anyone I know into the ground."

"Had enough practice in them fifty-seven years. I ain't like a machine. Instead of wearing out, more you use me, better I get."

When Chauncey had gotten up, he'd laid his Latin books on the homemade pine end table by his chair. Trig saw them there and asked what he'd been "a-studying" today. Trig always took an interest in his friend's endeavours and usually saw the rhyme, reason, and wherefore in Chauncey's choices to spend time.

Chauncey related his discovery of the two opposite words.

"An unploughed field. I'll second that," Trig said. "From that campus Clint went to, there was nothing tilled about that place, or tillable neither. Too much concrete. Too many sidewalks. A lot of cut over grass. Never seen such a busy squirrel warren web of asphalted roads. Never seen so many cars and parking garages and so much brick." Clint called the fancy parking buildings "garage-mahals." From the one time Trig had been there, he'd seen enough. "Wouldn't even make a decent cotton field, not to mention corn," he declared.

"Reckon they grow minds," Chauncey volunteered.

"From what Clint says, they're pitiful farmers then and grows mostly stunted nubbins. The full ears get that way mainly by themselves and despite the poor way the farmers farm."

Chauncey smiled. He liked the way Trig measured everything in one crop or another, particularly corn. "What you been up to today?" he asked.

"Been shellin' last year's dried corn with granddaddy's iron sheller. I finally fixed the hand crank and got it back to working again."

"Looks like you got a good crop put in again this year?"

"Yep."

"With your leftovers, you'll be farming in the woods once again, I reckon," Chauncey declared. "Well, it's a noble old tradition going back to old Ireland where your pa said all y'all Tinsleys come from."

Trig said Chauncey was right about where the family came from but couldn't just say what the Tinsleys had done over there. Probably mainly just fight the English landlords and starve. But it was too far back in time, over three hundred years, and, as he said, "I warn't there."

Trig sat down on a stool and thumbed through the Latin grammar. "Campus," he said aloud.

"You know, Chauncey, you've made a campus right here and in a ploughed field. Wonder if that wouldn't be the very best kind. Don't reckon those two words would have to be opposites, you know. Beneath them greying shucks, you've got a full ear. A row is judged by the crop it yields. Maybe not just today or tomorrow, but in the goodness of time."

Across the far hillside, they watched the clouds casting shadows as they moved. The checkerboard pattern on the landscape constantly shifted and played.

Chauncey went to his chores. Trig followed and helped when he could.

"Siller is sure a good milk cow. Just look at the cream," Trig said.

"Always liked Guernseys the best," Chauncey replied.

Trig commented on the neatness and energy of the poultry yard, as Chauncey broadcast some cracked corn.

"You sure have kept up this old farm well," Trig

complimented his friend. "All them bobwhites calling at the edge of the woods tell me everything I need to know."

Chauncey shared his simple supper with Trig. After a prayer blessing the food and remembering all those who'd gone before, they had ham, okra, fresh cucumbers, and red rice left over from dinner, still warm in the warming closet of the old cookstove. The basil was plentiful, and Chauncey had seasoned the red rice heavily with the herb.

"Good stuff!" Trig declared.

Biscuits, butter, sorghum molasses, and thick cream topped off the meal.

"This must be Mr. Attard Connelly's sorghum. I declare he makes some of the best. So good it'll make you slap your grandma. Nothing like a good sopping," Trig smacked his lips. Something in the honest way he did it kept it from being bad manners.

They sat on the porch in Chauncey's big rockers and talked of this and that, reminiscing at times back to childhood days.

"You know Trig, it's always a pleasure," Chauncey said to his friend. "When I talk to you, I don't have to explain each and every little thing. In your mind, you're already there. With some of those others, explaining more than talking and then as many times getting nowhere, wears a body out. Just no pleasure in trying to talk at all."

"I know," Trig agreed. "When we talk, things are lightened and cleared by what we already know. With them others, it's more like a long wrestling match, and never a winner in the ring. Takes forever and with no outcome. When it's over, feels like you've been in one of them ten-mile long iron-man marathons Clint talks about."

Chauncey nodded his head.

The heavy spring planter's moon began its rise.

"The moon's pouring water," Trig observed. "Soon going to rain."

Porch rockers creaked time with the rhythm of speech. After a space more, Trig said he had to be going on home. The two got in Chauncey's old truck, and the taillights began to show as it clanged its way down the lane, then up the hill to the gate at the road, through Chauncey's fields that last fall had yielded a better than usual harvest of gold and that were soon to be freshly ploughed once again in the cycle of things.

VIII
An Old Lesson

~⌇~

Triggerfoot was in a storytelling mood. This rainy spring day, on the lean-to porch outside Kildee's store, he had a big audience. The gathering was relaxed and there was nothing to rush them, nowhere they had to be, nothing pressing they had to do. The rain these past few days had made it too wet to plough, and Trig had already stuck cane poles to his half runners. They stood in neat tepees in eight straight rows.

"Enough to feed the countryside," Trig had declared, but he liked to carry messes around to his friends. It was one of those little things he could do, and folks appreciated it. But the beans weren't bearing quite yet, and he was taking some hours of leisure to catch up with news at the store.

Spurgeon Adams had been gassing on, boasting more than a bit, as was sometimes his way. He was having wife troubles. Seems that they'd been engaging in what Spurgeon called "pissing matches," and in that, he bragged, "You know how in that contest, nature has fixed it that men will always be bound to win."

So after more than enough of listening to the little details of little sparrings and petty contests, the assembled were somewhat relieved that Trig took advantage of a lull in the narrative to begin.

"Men, I got a story y'all gotta hear. I know I don't say it from experience, but I had this very tale from the oldest granddaddies of the oldest men. It's worth the hear.

"Yep. This story's so old it's as old as the people on earth. It happened way back, not too long, I reckon, after our old greatgrans Mr. Adam and Miss Eve came into the world."

"What's it about?" Spurgeon asked.

"Reckon it's about too much loose talk and not enough thinking with it," Trig replied. "A thing, one time or another, most of us are guilty of. Too much braggin', too much forgettin' what's the real centre of things. And usually leading to no good end.

"When a beautiful redheaded woman shows up at your hearth, you better just be thankful. And on your guard every day to remember the gift as the gift she is. I wasn't lucky enough to ever have such a one. I tried for it, but my perfect woman never would enter my old farmhouse door. Liked city life too well.

"This wasn't the case though with a chuckleheaded fellow named Cromer, a man who hadn't done a thing to deserve the woman named Marth. He hadn't even tried.

"Cromer was a typical enough fellow, nothing special about him—not too sharp, not too mindful of the favour he'd been shown. From childhood on, he wasn't a particularly hard-working fellow, but he wasn't exactly lazy neither, just sort of blindly stumbling along, too much interested in getting things the easy way, little business deals, little loaning out of money to get the interest off of, sort of like our famous old balloon collector Warn Pulliam, but set in the way-back times. He never felt like he ought to do too hard work tilling the fields and minding the flocks. All in all, he was a sorry lot, and no farmer much at all.

"No explanation for Marth. Appeared just out of nowhere without so much as a knock at the door. Came at dusk on a foggy grey day at the last of October, already turned cold. Wore a purple coat low about her milk-white shoulders, silver-edged and embroidered with twisted patterns of gold. Coat pinned with a round and sparkling jewel stickpin. Below her full bosoms, a tiny hugging place! Had beautiful shining long strawberry hair that shone in the sun.

"Just walked right in the open door, like she'd been there forever, and went straight to the fire. Started stirring the slim pot Cromer had put on. Didn't even look his way. They set down together and ate their meal. Still no word. When night came, she put everything in order without him asking her to, and went to his bed. She pulled back the blanket and just slipped right in beside him as smooth as silk. And with Cromer she stayed, no questions asked, no history explained. In all of this, even Cromer, who was known for the gift of gab, hadn't said a word.

"For week on week, Marth did Cromer's bidding as gentle, sweet, and loving a wife as was ever made. Never complained.

Never raised her voice or even murmured under her breath. There wasn't food or clothes needed, or anything else in her care. Weeks passed into months, months into seasons, and seasons into almost a year. Marth stayed steady, and Cromer kept up his not so industrious, yet still not lazy, ways.

"The folks around talked about Cromer's good luck, for the best of good luck, they reckoned it must be. No other way to explain it. He'd have been the last they'd have thought could have deserved it. They'd long figured him bland middle-of-the-road average in all things—or, truth to tell, a little below. His inches never had quite measured up to the norm. All he had was shrewdness in lending his few dollars and that's about all.

"A wise old man who'd followed the doings of Cromer and Marth made the comment that, for most of the community, summed up the scene. 'Even a blind hog gets an acorn once in awhile,' and the riddle was closed.

"But such a magical rare golden acorn Marth was to this blind common hog! Twenty-four carat, set with jewels and decorated with lacings and twinings of platinum.

"Cromer then got to blowing hard and bragging of the jewel he had. It didn't take long. And he did that after Marth had made him promise only one thing. 'I know I've been heart-devoted and given and comforted all that a person can, and that's worth more than the tallest mountain of gold and the highest claims in the land,' she'd said to Cromer. 'But of this, dear one, you must never brag.' This was her only demand, the only term of their deal, not to brag.

"So after a full four seasons of having all things big and small done for him just in this way, I reckon he got too proud in his good fortune, not having much else personally to be proud of. He forgot his promise and started to brag. He knew very well that his neighbours all envied him Marth, the couple's happiness and harmony, the smooth-running household she kept, and the fields of her tending, their fertile furroughs, their full orchards, and fat grazing flocks. In the flush of fortune, unknown before, Cromer forgot his wife's only command.

"And to top it all now, she was with child, no doubt a son.

"At the big harvest festival, one late fall morning, there were races held. King Conover, the most powerful man of the realm, as always won all the prizes that day. His horses took every race they entered upon. The crowd said there was nothing or no one could beat him. His men boasted and bragged. Cromer at the tavern that afternoon, after lifting a few, could hold his own in just one thing. He could hold his own with a brag.

"Lifting a great big mug, Cromer began: 'You think Conover's horses are fast? Well, let me tell you; my wife's faster. I got the best wife in the land. And that's a jewel worth more than the king's gold-beaten crown. If I'd tell her, she'd run swifter than the best of Conover's horses and easily put them to shame. She'd do what I'd say without even a frown. How many of you men can say the same. Not even the king!'

"There at the tavern that afternoon were some of King

Conover's men. They were also lifting a mug or two. A little wobbly, they took Cromer's boast straight to Conover's door. Straightway, Conover had Cromer marched to the big castle house under guard of six men, the very next hour—so swift was Conover's justice and how deeply he resented the slight.

"He told Cromer that if his wife didn't run the next race tomorrow and win, Cromer would be hanged quicker than the king's own horses could run. Cromer started shaking and fell to the floor. What a pretty mess he'd got himself into!

"Cromer was taken under guard to his once happy home; and, all startled, Marth met him at the door.

"She said hello to him with only two words: 'You've bragged.' She didn't have to question. She knew.

"'Oh, don't ask it,' she answered as the request was made. Marth was showing extra big with his child. Everybody said she was so big it must be twins.

"To Conover and court next morning, she made her plea. 'A mother bore each of you men. Defend me, I beg. Only wait till my child that kicks so strong inside of me is born.' But she couldn't move them at all. Not the cold heart of a single one. And so vain was Conover, so puffed up with pride that he shouted a thundering '*No*! Win the race or this man dies! Your husband should learn to curb his tongue. He should know where he is and who he is and his place in the world.'

"Many there knew that Conover's queen was a real battle-ax and often wore the pants, and sometimes even the crown, of the realm. Conover's men snickered over this and mumbled, when they were sure Conover wasn't around, that this whole thing with Cromer came out of Conover's jealousy. Thought Conover: 'What a wife like Cromer's would be worth in silver, jewels, and gold, in flocks and herds of animals, in miles and miles of orchards and fertile ploughed land!'

"But Conover wouldn't back down. Pale as a ghost, and speechless for once, Cromer stood.

"Then Marth appealed one last time to the men of the realm, men born of mothers like she'd soon be, but even big tears in her gentle blue eyes didn't move a single heart of stone.

"So child in her belly, and true to her husband and to save him from death, she ran the race and with the last ounce of her strength, she won. Her husband was free, but she fell in the dust in labour the minute she nudged the finish line. Two beautiful blond sons were born, but the mother died.

"With her last breath, she cursed King Conover and all the men who'd shown her no pity that day—all men down to the ninth generation to come. The curse went this way:

"'Whenever you'll be in your worst trouble, you'll suffer pangs keener than birth pangs, and sharper-toothed than my own, and lasting three and thirty days. You'll be so used up, you'll be prey for any who'll walk your way. Weak as a newborn, motherless kitten, you'll be, and defenseless as baby bird with unopened eye.'

"That day, hearing her, many a stout heart shook with fear. And the curse came to pass. It fell to every corner of the land. In no fold of the hills, no furthest tucked away place could you hide, but it followed you there. And Cromer, spared his life, died by his cold hearth alone, a dried up old man with an empty pot on its hook, and a house as empty of joy as it had been before Marth had showed up at his door. His sons, knowing the story of how their mama died, left him as soon as they were old enough and could."

His tale finished, Trig didn't look over at Spurgeon, and neither did his friends. But he sat sober enough, faking a look of not having figured any of this might pertain to him.

When Chauncey got home later that evening, he said to himself, "Maybe old Trig did some good today." And he wished it sincerely, for Spurgeon, imperfect as he was in so many ways, was still a neighbour and friend.

"And if it didn't," Chauncey thought as he yawned, and turned over onto his side in the bed, "It was a rattling good tale."

"Old Triggerfoot, now he's an original," he said under his breath. Through closed eyes out of the *spiritus mundi* he could see a lovely golden mare with hooves planted firmly on the ground. Standing beside her was a pair of golden-haired boys. The mare was decked out splendid in shining red and silver, circle-patterned silks, and all behind her was the sun and a tall field of bright tasselled corn.

"*Tuatha-da-danaan,*" he said aloud to the dark in the Irish Gaelic he was trying to learn. It was coming more naturally than Latin. He said the words again as his thoughts dissolved into sleep and the light of the full planter's moon fell upon his unclad body tired from honest toil. Its beams moved aslant his bed, then made silver twisting patterns that danced their mysterious jigs on the foot-polished floor.

Outside a mocking bird vied with the whippoorwills, spring peepers, and tree frogs to celebrate the promise of the ripening spring.

IX

Moss and Mould

~ ❧ ~

Across the potbellied stove came more comment than question: "When are you ever going to paint that old farmhouse of yours!" It was addressed to Triggerfoot, who'd allowed a break in the conversation at Cousin Kildee's store, a thing he didn't often do. The speaker was a smart-alecky fellow who didn't know Triggerfoot that well, or he wouldn't have ventured to say.

"When hell freezes over and you the biggest icicle hanging on its wall," came the reply quick as a shot.

Chauncey had to chuckle at his friend, and now he couldn't resist egging him on.

"I declare Trig, the moss and mould are about to take you over, to seal up your doors and windows where you can't get out or in. Wonder it doesn't get to you in your bed in summer on one of these humid, wet nights and seal up your mouth and eyes."

"*Mould, smould*!" answered Triggerfoot. "What's wrong with moss and mould, I'd like to know."

"Nothing, if you're the north side of a tree or a rock," Spurgeon Adams declared.

"Or the forest floor," Chauncey volunteered.

"Just so it ain't on my gravestone," Lyman Eppes halfway agreed. He was in his eighties and could easily foresee that day.

"Well, I consider the little mossies and mouldies to be just my particular friends," answered Triggerfoot after a pause. "I like them especially well on a rose-colored brick wall. It makes that brick a lot less mechanical hard and more than a building material you get down yonder in Columbia at Lowe's or Home Depot. Some time when you can slow down from your getting and spending, Spurgeon Adams, just sit there and look at it. See what you can see."

"Then they'd sure think we're crazy around here, them hurrying folks in Clay Bank town," Adams replied.

"Yep," agreed Mr. Lyman. "They already say that around here we've got nothing more exciting to do than watch the paint peel."

"What paint!" exclaimed Triggerfoot. "Thought y'all were just now saying my house needed it. And I thought we were talking about mould."

At old Mr. Lyman's last comment, Kildee looked up from the counter and inserted his favourite expression about his community. "I like to think of this place as a regular hotbed of tranquility. Watching paint peel would be too tiring and way too strenuous for me."

"You done got me off the subject," interrupted Trig. "Pardon me if I'm wrong . . . I believe I was speaking of the pleasantness of mould."

"Sit there or stand, take your choice," he continued. "But

look over yonder at that brick wall. As the cool of a shadow, then the warm of the sun will hit it, see what you'll see. The brick gets mellowed by green, mellow like the taste of my best corn liquor or good five-year-old scuppernong wine."

"True," Chauncey agreed. "I know exactly what you mean. It looks like brush strokes on a painting, or a fine antique tapestry that's hung on a wall."

Trig continued, "Spurgeon Adams, the result might surprise you and it's this humble green mould's done the job, made a kind of harmony, like fiddle and banjo does to a song."

"Alchemy," Chauncey added. "Green come out of time."

Trig warmed to his subject: "I like the thin green of mould and mosses on that old unpainted silver wood of my house like I like it here on Kildee's store. It shows it wasn't built just yesterday."

"How old is your house anyway, Triggerfoot?" the stranger inquired.

"Don't rightly know. Old enough, I reckon. It's been there at least two hundred years. My great-great-great-grandpappy built it from oak, pine, and poplar cut from off the place. The stairs are solid walnut from trees off the hill."

"The original old forest wood," added Mr. Lyman. "That won't rot in a day like this sorry soft pine they grow on their sorry-arse tree farms."

"True it is," Chauncey agreed. "I'll bet stuff built from that pitiful wood won't last two hundred years."

"Lucky to last two," Kildee replied.

"Yep. That's what I like about mould," Trig came back to

his subject again. "When I see it, wherever I see it, a peace steals into me like the best of the old ballad songs."

"Peace!" declared Adams, not following Trig's meanderings there.

"Yep. *Peace*, Spurgeon Adams," answered Trig. "Peace because moss comes only when things've stayed put and proved true by lasting a long time, where folk remember back a piece."

The thought settled awhile around the cold stove. For a long while, no one ventured a word at that, sensing the good sense of the thing. Chauncey thought to himself that Japanese gardeners would certainly understand Trig, and he did too.

That's what Chauncey particularly liked about his friend. He'd plumb-out startle you sometimes with things you ought to know already, and maybe did, but hadn't brought to the front of your mind.

But for some, in other places and situations, startle was not the word. Trig with his truths had been known to upset more than a stuffy, hypocritical few, and in mighty high places at that. And for his revealing their scams, he'd felt their punishment's sting. Of this, Trig had once remarked to his friend. "You know, Chauncey," he'd said. "Truth's a mighty good dog, but he better watch out barking too close to the heels of a lie, lest he get his brains kicked in."

The pause continued. Then it was Trig himself who broke silence and picked up the trail.

"Yep. Lasted," he said. "No telling what in them two

centuries the thing's endured. Toil and tumult, blood and giving, have gone to its make, sweat and brave deeds and dreams of heroes, little and big. I reckon the old dry wood itself has soaked up sacrifice and tears, and sometimes blood, and it's come out in green."

"Like memory," Chauncey declared. "When you're around old things enough, you remember better, that's sure. Those scientists whose ways rule the world would have us believe time's like an arrow, linear progressive, shot into the endless future, they'd say. But a little simple thing like memory puts the lie to that way. It can swirl time and make it all one. Time's what the mind makes it, and memory jumps about and plays hell with the scientist's way. That's why this efficient new world doesn't like to remember, and hates and scorns us with memories too. Where there's mould and moss, seems easier to remember. Around them two, the generations are known to each other and get linked up, each to each. By the time you get to be over half a century, like all of us here, we're likely to have known four or five generations of any family—most particularly our own. We're just our ancestors in our own time."

Kildee added, "I've always thought that for every child that comes across the threshold of this old store, it's interesting to guess what he'll become. Will he take after his daddy's line? Or maybe his grandpa on his mama's side? I've usually known 'em all. He's not just a child, but an old friend brought into a new time. An old friend or relative in small."

"Yep. Right you are Kildee," Mr. Lyman picked up the thread. "And you'll most likely know so many things about him that he'll never even know about himself."

The men around the store thought about the truth of that and wondered just what eighty-one-year-old Mr. Lyman knew about them that they'd never know.

Mr. Lyman correctly intuited their thoughts.

"And I ain't tellin'," he said with a laugh.

"Lots of us already remember way too much," Kildee declared. "And we're not that old. In the big cities, it's said they live for the moment and hurry about, forgetting yesterday as quick as a year. Round here, nobody ever forgets a single damn solitary thing. It's always passed down. Dern if it ain't! Ain't nothin' allowed to die when there's so many storytellers around, and all of us are."

"My gentle, sweet wife," added Mr. Lyman, "Bless her soul, were she still here, would agree with you there, friend Kildee. Before she died at age eighty, she told me she was ready to go because she just remembered too much."

Chauncey said sadly, "It takes a long time to build up that storehouse of wisdom, richer than any bank, and knowing about things that matter the most. Then it's all gone in an eye-blink, unless we get and hold it to pass on. Sometimes stories are the only way, and usually the best. Some of the most important things I know about this place came from stories told me by old ladies. I hate so bad when a one of them goes. But in other places, seems like old ladies have gone out of style."

"Old codgers, too," said Mr. Lyman. "Like me. I oughta know. But I never was up with the times or in fashion, even when I was three."

Because no one around the stove was old enough to know him when he was three, none of them even thought to venture a comment to that, not even Triggerfoot or Kildee, both of whom were never known to be short of words.

"Well, Mr. Lyman, you're such a character," Adams declared. "At least we won't take you for granted, in fashion or out. And characters themselves ain't in fashion in many places any more either."

Chauncey shook his head and shifted his weight in his cane-bottomed chair. The canes crackled with his motion. "I used to be afraid that all the characters would die out around here," he said. "Because most of them were old and dropping by the way."

Chauncey paused a long pause.

"And?" Triggerfoot finally inquired. He knew that's what Chauncey was fishing to hear. To be asked peaked the listeners' interest. It was part of the taleteller's art to draw out such a question, and Chauncey was learning from the masters he heard every day.

"And . . . well . . . they haven't! As soon as one goes and we say the place'll never be quite the same ever again, no more colour left, the likes of him never more to be seen, then up starts another, sprouting eccentricities as quickly and easily as corn after a warm rain."

"Ec-cen-tricities, you say, Chauncey, 'specially the sin part from what I see." Triggerfoot couldn't resist the play on words.

"I wonder, Trig, if you're not now accounted a character your own self hereabouts," Kildee ventured in a deadpan way.

"Instead of character, I'd rather be one of them eccentrics, with that emphasis on *sin*," Trig replied.

Adams, who was usually the one most likely to have another place to be and in a hurry to get there, was once again the first to break the charm and mention he must leave.

"Got to get going," he said. His chair scraped the floor and his footsteps kept time with the old eight-day clock on the shelf.

He was gone with the very first mention of going, unlike the usual case with the rest of the men, who'd say it at least three times and just hold their ground.

For as the men intuited, crossing the threshold either in or out was a charm of its own, and not to be lightly considered before performance set in. The threshold divided two worlds. Styx, Charon, that old hound Cerberus, and even Jordan had nothing on it.

The threshold beyond this threshold of their mossy world tapestried with the alchemy of green was mostly invisible to them, but as clearly demarked, as starkly delineated as the lines of milk-white quartz in the local granite or mica in the dark stone.

"Reckon the world will ever catch up to us?" Triggerfoot inquired of his friends.

"Not likely," answered Chauncey. "They're just so far ahead, they're behind. They've broken all the treaties with nature and the oldest covenants with God. They scorn the man sweating in the fields, with his patience and harmony with things. They've got no real kinship with us anymore. And we're so far behind, we're ahead, but the others don't have a clue. In all of this, then, who's smart and who's dumb?"

There was a pause at the gravity of this.

"Men are most surely going to starve when they quit planting the soil," Mr. Lyman agreed. "It's the oldest partnering folks can remember, if remember they ever do nowadays."

A pause and Triggerfoot shook his head. "And if that ain't the worst thing," he declared. "It'll do till the worst thing comes along."

These solemn thoughts hung heavy at the stove. The ceiling's naked light bulb, as was its way, seemed to get brighter as the day waned. Mr. Lyman nodded briefly in sleep. He woke himself, startled, with his own slumping down in the chair. When he looked around, he first had to think where he was. "Eighty-one years," he said. "Like my wife, guess I just remember too much. Maybe, like her, it's time I was gone."

"We'd miss you sorely. You know we would," Kildee answered. "If only for our sakes, hold on."

"Yes, I'd hate for there to be no character left around here," he replied with a chuckle. "The world would sure be painted up neat and tidy all in only one new shining coat of the same colour, probably cheery yellow like a false sunshine or like that squeaky-clean dish detergent they advertise. Everything would be all prim and proper, ruler drawn. All neat and at efficient right angles. Nothing ramshackled and shaklety. No moss. No mould."

Trig smiled at Mr. Lyman's irony, and all four of them let the quiet come down as a benediction, so that Mr. Lyman could go back to his doze.

X

On Time

The moment of the day so small Satan can't find it is when the poet's work is done.

—William Blake

It was just past what the old folks called busting out the middles time, when the furroughs between the young growing crops were ploughed to kill weeds and loosen the soil's crust. It was now lay by time, and there was a little slack space before pulling corn and picking cotton would begin. These days allowed some breathing room for the men of the community to visit Kildee's store. Today, there were half a dozen assembled there. They noticed two men they didn't know crossing the old threshold.

"No A.C.?" one of the strangers said incredulously to the other, as they came inside. It was half question and declaration at the same time. He didn't seem to care if he'd be heard.

His partner, a bit more circumspect, answered him in a whisper, "Can you believe it! I didn't think there was any place of business left anywhere in the world that could get away with that."

The man made it sound like Kildee was committing some kind of crime, getting away with some heinous violation.

The two men had come to the store to offer Kildee a great deal, "the deal of his life." They promised it would save him a whole lot of money. Their attitude was that the locals should thank them for coming.

Kildee had looked up just in time to see their shiney new vehicle drive up in a hurry out front. Its door sported the words "VANDALLA'S AMERICAN VINYL SIDING" in great patriotic red, white, and blue block letters. There was even a U.S. flag painted by the words. As Kildee had figured, they were from the Columbia branch of a big national company and were out drumming up business in the rural communities where there were a lot of old frame buildings—farmhouses and structures like Kildee's store. He'd guessed their game before they came in the door.

Chauncey also saw the men pull up. He was chatting with Uncle Dick Gilliam (pronounced *Gill-um* in this part of the world) who was sitting in a big high-back rocker next to him. He was just poised to tell Chauncey a tale.

Uncle Dick was an elderly black gentleman who lived alone in a cabin his granddaddy had built on the high banks of the Broad River many years ago. It hadn't been written down, but he reckoned he was at least eighty-one or eighty-two, about the same age as Mr. Lyman, they surmised. As he said, it didn't bother him none not knowing, for when you got that old, what's a year or two in the scheme of things. He didn't do much anymore, but time still didn't weigh heavy on his hands.

He was making one of his rare visits to the store. His river home was a good ten miles off. Uncle Dick had no car—in fact, couldn't drive, had never driven one. He did his travelling on the river, and couldn't do much of that anymore. So he didn't get up that way often, or for that matter, anywhere else either. He made it to Seekwell A. M. E. Church every Sunday and stayed all day, and that was now usually the sum total of his contact with society.

When he did come to Kildee's, it was a keen pleasure for all, for Uncle Dick was one of the best storytellers around. If you could time it just right and coax him the right way to tell a tale, you were in for a real treat. Today, Chauncey had had the leisure to go down after him and bring him up to the store.

Chauncey and Uncle Dick stopped their conversation to observe the city men. They were opening the heavy lid of the giant drink cooler and commenting on the coldness of the drink bottles nestled down in the ice. "The only cool thing around here," one said to the other. "I could sure use something cool." The ice made a sloshing sound as they went in after their choices. To their consternation, there were no beers.

The strangers each got them a Co-cola and instead of putting the money in the can by the cooler, paid Kildee. They introduced themselves and went straight into a pitch to sell the company's wares. Carmine, the tall one, handed around his business card. Chauncey noticed the company's motto: "One Size Fits All."

"You'll never need a paint brush again," Carmine began. "It makes time stand still."

"Or ever buy another gallon of paint," his sidekick said, backing him up. "The best that new age technology can provide." His name was Gene. His jacket had an embroidered label on the chest reading "INSTALLATION TECHNICIAN."

Chauncey looked at Uncle Dick. Uncle Dick looked at Chauncey.

Speaking so as not to be heard by the visitors, Uncle Dick said, "But this old place ain't *never* been painted anyway, far as I know."

Chauncey nodded his head in agreement and smiled. "Never will either, if I know Kildee."

"Vinyl insulates and protects from storm," said Carmine. "Our company and team of trained technicians can put in storm windows and storm doors too. Make everything airtight, nice and snug, neat and tidy as neat and tidy can be. Can do it for one money, can give you a package deal. Can do it on time, on our installment plan. Easy monthly payments we can arrange."

While Carmine talked, Gene pulled out a slick folder of coloured pictures to show what they could and would do. They had eight models of glass storm doors.

Uncle Dick looked at Chauncey again. "With them fancy

glass doors, 'spect Mr. Kildee wouldn't know how to act. Nor would the dogs and cats, I reckon, who come and go as they please without no door. They wouldn't any more. Like me, Mr. Kildee ain't never even had a screen door before, much less a glass one too."

"Guess them dogs and cats would have to learn how to knock or mash a door bell," Chauncey replied.

"Buying on time," Uncle Dick said. "And if Mr. Kildee didn't make them easy monthly payments each month on time, that there Vandalla Company might be owning what use to be his store. I done learned that lesson the hard way over fifty years ago."

But Carmine, acting as if he hadn't heard Uncle Dick, said, "You wouldn't believe how our vinyl siding and storm doors and windows can make a place airtight. You wouldn't believe how much they'd cut down on heating and cooling costs. We always estimate that they pay for themselves in fuel savings in less than five years."

This time Chauncey looked at Uncle Dick.

After a pause, Uncle Dick observed, "Mr. Chauncey, when you don't have heating and cooling costs, how can it cut down?"

"Beats me, Uncle Dick," was Chauncey's reply. "I reckon next step would be to get central heat and air so's the siding would pay for itself, and you could make sure you were getting your money's worth for having put it in. Bet you could get that on time too."

"Hah! Mr. Chauncey. Very like!" Uncle Dick resisted the inclination to grunt.

Kildee said he reckoned he'd wait awhile before he'd use the services of VANDALLA'S VINYL SIDING AND STORM WINDOWS & DOORS. ONE SIZE FITS ALL, but thanked them just the same. Then because he was in a mischievous mood today, he set Carmine and Gene onto Chauncey, knowing very well what Chauncey would feel about having vinyl siding and storm windows and doors installed at his old house. He wished Triggerfoot was there, but Chauncey would have to do.

"This here's Chauncey Doolittle," Kildee said. "He lives in a big old two-storey house that's needing paint. Why don't you help him. See if your one size can fit him." Kildee looked over at Chauncey and smiled.

Chauncey ignored him but nodded at the two men.

So the pair drew up two chairs by Chauncey, and this time it was Kildee who observed.

Carmine went through his drill, sounding like a recording.

At the airtightness business, Chauncey asked, "Isn't that bad for wood?"

Carmine looked like someone had cussed in church. Chauncey had just offended the sacredness of the new-age product he sold. Of course, Chauncey was right, and that's why Carmine had to look hurt. What else could he do?

"On, no, Mr. Doolittle, it keeps the rain out," he said.

"Or house moisture *in*," Chauncey replied. Although Chauncey knew very well the effects of vinyl siding on wood frame buildings, he didn't go into details. He figured the salesmen were very much aware of that too.

Still ignoring Chauncey's comment, Carmine went on, "It's a miracle product, the result of progress in science. State of the art. Impervious to wet. Resistant to fire. There's no element it can't subdue. Our team of scientist experts are bringing miracles right to your door. The very latest and best."

"Sounds like they're bringing us the door too," Uncle Dick grunted to Chauncey.

"I'm not ready for that kind of miracle," Chauncey replied. "But thank you just the same."

To that, Carmine didn't know exactly what to say, but as usual, undaunted, he went on. He'd given this spiel so many times he could just put it on automatic pilot, Cadillac cruise control.

He didn't forget to use the feature of last resort, his ace up his sleeve, his highest trump card. "And all on the installment plan too, Mr. Doolittle. No money down. Installment of vinyl on the installment plan. A perfect match and fit! We can adjust the size to fit every bank account, no matter how small."

"What bank account?" Uncle Dick mumbled to himself.

While Carmine talked, Gene asked Kildee, "Where's your restroom?"

"Out back," Kildee replied. Gene didn't make a move in the direction pointed. He must have decided he could wait.

Chauncey listened Carmine out to the end, then firmly, courteously, said no. He didn't want Carmine and Gene to look at his home. He didn't want it measured. He didn't want a free estimate of the cost, no obligations incurred. He didn't want a schedule of monthly payments on time. He didn't want a free computer-graphics picture of how his house would look with the vinyl siding on or the various colours it could be in. He didn't want a printout of how much savings in heating and cooling costs it would bring. Like Kildee, he had no central heat or A.C.

The two salesmen departed to peddle their expert miracle product door to door, hoping to get some gullible farmer to bite at their shiney new fish lure. As Carmine summed up to Gene as they walked to their car, "We should have known it would have been nothing but a complete waste of time from the minute we walked in there. Did you take a good look at the place? Man!"

The store had had time to get quiet again. After relishing silence awhile, Chauncey volunteered, "The joys of sales resistance. The consumerist, planned-obsolescent society whipped at least one time today."

"Never have wanted to live in a Tupperware container or a Glad bag!" Kildee declared.

"Me neither," Uncle Dick replied. "Don't know where this progress is to take us to. I can't get my breath in sealed-up places like that. That's all I know. Don't want no coffin before I have to."

Kildee pulled up a rocker and sat with the two.

"They say it's progress how we can grow wood so fast today on these new pine-tree farms. Maximum profit for minimum outlay that way. No time wasted in cashing in from your outlay. But the wood's so soft and sorry, it rots unless it's got protection from the rain. So the progress we get is copper naphthenate and other chemical wood preservatives from the chemical plants, and they say that in time the stuff causes cancer in those who puts it on and has it around. Then that's outlawed. Progress again. So progress next is to make plastic containers to put buildings in."

There was a pause. It was Chauncey's turn. "So now we find that having houses sealed up so tight is real bad for them who live in them. Radon gas now. And, on top of that, the vinyl rots down the house from inside."

Kildee picked up his original thread, "So if we didn't have that progressive, cost-effective, get-rich-quick, rushed way of growing wood in the first place, we wouldn't need all that other progress that leads to death in some, and to all a dead end. The old slow-growing heart pine that this store's made out of, oozes so much resin, it'll never rot. Any termite brave enough to tackle it dulls its teeth."

"Smells good too," Chauncey agreed. "Like a clean-smelling old-growth forest, it's good for the lungs. The wood's had time to grow at its ease. Nobody rushing it along. Triggerfoot says the smell of pine resin and pine needles makes him feel so good, he wants to snort."

Then the three sat quiet awhile. Chauncey was marvelling at the absurdity of rushing everything in a way to destroy life, and of all what the world so in love with fads and science and technology called the new improved and progressive ways. He kept remembering his daddy's saying when Chauncey would be hurrying about, that he ought to slow down, the world wasn't made in a day. "Took six, I believe," he'd declare. Chauncey could hear him like it was yesterday.

"Mr. Kildee," Uncle Dick finally broke the silence. "Sounds to me like you'll not be getting that vinyl siding put on here any time soon."

"Don't reckon I will, Uncle Dick," Kildee replied. "How about you?"

"Wasn't asked, I reckon you saw," Uncle Dick replied. "They looked right through me. I figured they've X-rayed me with their progress eyes and didn't see no fat pocketbook inside this old coat. All that talk about bank accounts didn't include Uncle Dick. Reckon they didn't have time for the likes of me."

Chauncey chuckled at that. "You reckon the improved eyes of progress can X-ray, Uncle Dick?" he asked.

"Wouldn't be surprised, Mr. Chauncey," Uncle Dick replied. "You know they've walked on the moon, are sending things up to Mars. But I still lives on the banks of old man Broad, and I still gets along just fine without the likes of them or their kind knowing I'm even there. They know all these other things from atoms to Mars and the moon, but they don't know me. And I'm just tickled pink I's invisible to them and their kind."

"Their loss, not yours," Kildee observed.

"Progress of the seasons, Mr. Kildee, is progress enough for me. You can tell the time of the year on the face of the mighty man. That river's not changed in its changes that way in my eighty some years. No progress there, and that's the pattern for me. I got no time for the rushing world. We's like two brothers, that river and me, or more like pappy and son. He was there before Grandpap and will be there long after me. He's a right steady friend. He's got all the time in the world to keep me company. I lives most of the time outside of door, abiding with him. Constant, that's what he is, and so will I be, till Old Master calls me home. Let me tell y'all one thing I'se learned in my eight decades of life," he continued after a pause.

For that, the whole room got quiet as birds in the woods at the moment before rain. Kildee looked up from the package he was tying with string. Chauncey turned his face from the door.

"Well, it's just that the littlest minds of all get wrapped up in the biggest things, and that the biggest minds always sees the special in the least little dooryard things."

With that, Uncle Dick rose carefully to his feet and adjusted his weight to balance himself on his carved cedar cane.

It was late evening now, time to shut up the store and go home. Chauncey walked Uncle Dick out to the truck, opened the truck door, and helped him inside. Now maybe on their ride home he'd have time to get that tale the vinyl-siding salesmen had broken off when they walked in the door. When they showed up, Uncle Dick had just said, "'Minds me of the time when the river . . ." Chauncey regretted that most of all. "What a waste," he thought to himself. "Like replacing wood with plastic, the loss of the genuine real to the fake and the sham."

Chauncey knew that Uncle Dick's best stories always involved in some way the river outside his door—his father, brother, and constant friend—and he figured this story was going to be one of them too. This made the loss even bitterer to bear. All Uncle Dick's stories were memorable, no matter the subject or theme. They taught Chauncey lessons he'd be hard-pressed to learn on even the best pages of men. So, yes, today he'd drive extra slow taking Uncle Dick home. He'd even take the long way round.

XI

Field Trip: The Devil on Highway 34

The year was passing in earnest now. It was well past lay-by time and full square in the green-shuck days, a season for pulling the young sweet corn that folks called "roastin' ears." Chauncey gloried in the activity, and this year had yielded a particularly good crop.

Green-shuck time always put Triggerfoot in high spirits. It's a good thing too because Kildee's store had needed some livening up these past weeks. There seemed to be a general funk about the place the cause for which no one could quite figure.

Seems that Triggerfoot's friend Flop-Eye's son had gone on the wagon, this time for sure, or at least the son claimed. He hadn't touched a drop in over a month, not even a beer. As for the occasional "recreational drug" that punctuated his young life with high holidays, he wouldn't even hear of it, not even when it was free and reported to be the purest, absolute best.

"Why come?" Lyman Eppes asked Trig.

Triggerfoot gave the paused, settled look of hunkering down that Chauncey knew always announced a tale about to be told. Chauncey also sat back, relaxed, preparing himself to relish the telling like some would anticipate brandy or fine Cuban cigars after a fancy meal.

Triggerfoot began right in without any of his usual preparatory hemming and hawing and circuitous delayings.

"Y'all know Mr. Val Lyles over there in Fairfield. Him that we call the Mayor of Salem Crossroads, population twelve. Well, this tale involves him."

"But we thought it was about your friend's son, and him going on the wagon," Chauncey interrupted just to arouse Triggerfoot's ire.

"I'll get there. Just give me time. I got my ways. You got to know Val Lyles first to know how come all this come about.

"Well, Mr. Val had started to raising buffalo because there's of late a great city craze for buffalo steaks. He's tried this and that to keep the farm afloat, and that's been hard with so many things these days working to nail nail-holes into the ship's hull, not to mention a near fatal run or two onto sharp rocks at the bank.

"His latest plan to bail and sell pine straw to city folks through the garden center in Clay Bank didn't work out. So Val decided he'd give buffalo a try. Yes, he'd tried about everything else from llamas to lespedeza, from soybeans to sunflower seeds.

"He got him a big bull buffalo, which he straightway, of course, named Buffalo Bill. Val surrounded Bill with a dozen or so of the young enticing female kind. It was buffalo heaven on earth for Bill. Soon the little calf buffalos started to arrive so regularly that Val had got him a regular herd.

"Well, one thing about buffalo nature is they won't be fenced in. They like to rove and roam."

"Sort of like you, Trig," Kildee volunteered with a wry smile.

"Damn straight!" Triggerfoot replied.

"Well Val couldn't keep Big Bill, the cows, and the young'uns inside his fenced-in fields. No matter what he'd do, he couldn't keep them in. Sort of like the impossible way you can't keep deer out of a black-eyed-pea field or a peanut patch. So out they'd get, especially at night, and out they'd rove around, taking their ease.

"Now, this brings us to my friend Flop-Eye's boy, Marquis."

"You've told us about Marquis once before," Kildee declared. "He's the one you asked Flop-Eye about his name."

"Yep, I thought it might be some family name way back, but old Flop-Eye, cocking that one good owl eye at me, said, 'No, Mr. Triggerfoot, I laid with his mam in a Mercury Marquis and that's how Marquis got into the world.'

"So," Trig continued, "Marquis had reached a restless nineteen, and couldn't be managed. He was a lot like that buffalo herd. Flop-Eye did try to keep him at home of a Saturday night, but no matter what, he'd sneak out when Flop-Eye and the missus would nod off to sleep.

"Marquis had him a favorite roughneck night spot some few miles from home, and there he'd go of a Saturday night. The

Purple Palace was a concrete block thirty-by-twenty single room. It was painted purple inside and out. Its windows were plywooded up and painted purple too, so what went on inside stayed inside. It had the reputation of a place you could get cut up. No white man had ever come in its doors and most of the black folks were about afraid to too.

"This particular Saturday night about a month ago, Marquis was about as high as crystal meth and Crown Royal would get him and he'd had him a few good snorts of coke to boot, so he was feeling no pain, and generally obstropolous in spreading himself around.

"His best buddy Quinticious had him a new shiney black Pontiac Firebird with purple front neon fluorescent bumper lights and oversize spinner wheels, and they turned on their rap music and went out for a spin.

"Well, who should they meet on the dark lonely road but Big Bill and his herd, plumb in the middle of the road.

"If you know the buffalo, you'll know their eyes ain't like deer. Deer eyes in the headlights make a greenish glow. Buffaloes make a firecoal red.

"Marquis, Quinticious, and the boys come face to face, head to head, with Big Bill. The windshield warn't more than ten foot from Bill's eyes. What with the glaring red, his horns and long shaggy goatee beard, Marquis vowed he'd seen the devil hisself, complete with the devil's active working crew.

"Them spinner-cap tires reversed and spun and smoked, and Quinticious backed his way at sixty mph, till they got away from there."

Chauncey's eyes grew as wide as Mr. Lyman's and Kildee's. Then they broke into a good laugh.

"Reckon the devil never looked more like the devil than Big Bill through an alcohol haze on a high lonesome road," contributed Spurgeon Adams, who'd sat quietly through all of this. He chuckled out loud.

"Well, Flop-Eye says Marquis swore off liquor, women, and all carousing around that very night. And he's been true to his promise, faithfully, religiously true, to this day. Even started going to Seekwell A. M. E. Like his grandma made him do as a child."

"The Lord works in mysterious ways," Mr. Lyman declared. "Maybe that's what it would take to dry old Triggerfoot out."

"Not likely," declared Triggerfoot after a pause. "It would take more than the devil to separate me from my jug. But as for that wacky weed, them funny little merry-widder cigarettes, crystal Methodists, and cocaine, I can leave all that truck along. The smoke of a good Cuban cigar is about all I wants to go up my nose.

There was a long silence.

"'Specially them crystal Methodists," Kildee declared. "After what happened to you and old Flop-Eye." They all knew every detail of that story of going to church with the Methodists, and chuckled at the recollection. Nobody needed filling in or reminding.

Then it was Bob Graham who broke the silence. He communicated that it seems Big Bill was also the centre of one more occasion of confusion in the community. This time, Bo Keitt, a neighbour up the road some miles, was the one to meet up with Big Bill and the herd.

"Well, Bo was out on a tear over yonder in Winnsboro," Mr. Bob related. "And he was coming home to his long-suffering wife late one moonless night back this spring when he ran his little Toyota truck smack into the herd. Big Bill, as usual, had run down the fences and was onto the highway.

"With his reflexes dulled, Bo grazed a cow pretty hard and messed up the front of his truck. When he finally got home, the missus asked him what had happened. He was bummed up a little, a jammed finger and a bloody nose from hitting the windshield, but mainly still half drunk.

"Course he answered her he'd run into a herd of buffalo on the way home. Nothing would stop Mrs. Keitt from taking Bo to the emergency room, thinking he had a concussion and was delusional."

"I'd heard tell something of that," added Adams. "And it's a wonder wrecking that little truck that way didn't kill Bo graveyard dead."

"Chaunts, old boy, now what would you do if you met Big Bill of a dark night on a high lonesome tear?" Trig asked his friend.

"Well, Trig, I don't rightly know. I'll have to think about that awhile. Maybe I'll sleep on it—take a little nap right here in this chair, and then let you know."

To tell the truth, under the influence of the afternoon's heat and the store's tin roof, several in the building had already dozed off. One even snored. Some one of them had joked that the fellow's mouth over yonder by the door was open so wide that a fly could go in and out without being disturbed.

Then followed a long patch of quiet, interrupted only by the passing of cats and dogs, time enough for the assembled crew to think about Trig's and Graham's tales and take all their ramifications in.

As for Trig himself, he showed himself contented as a man could be.

Kildee noticed Trig's well-being and his joy abounding. Commenting to Chauncey, Kildee pronounced his old friend happy as a petted puppy with two peters.

At this, Chauncey had to laugh at the homely rightness of the phrase. Then all fell quiet again as the slow evening shadows grew longer and began to cool the good land.

XII
Honky-Tonk Recess

It was hotter than hot. The dog days had set in, and at night, Sirius blazed in the cloudless sky. Today at the store, the men sat around, or, more accurately, drooped.

There were Lyman Eppes, Chauncey, and two men in their late twenties from out of the county, all sitting in the store's centre, farthest from the sun and where there was some cross ventilation. Not much breeze blew through though. One of the strangers was from Boykin, the other from Antioch, two rural communities about forty miles away. They worked as linemen for the REA and were taking off some time to sit, and listen mostly.

Kildee was not at his usual place behind the polished wood counter, but himself also sat in a rocker. He was a bit down. The heat had affected him these last few weeks. He was in an undershirt, a rare sight at the store.

"Oh, you're just stove up from all that farm work," Mr. Lyman volunteered.

"Reckon I'm just getting old," Kildee surmised. "Hot

weather use never to bother me at all. Of late, seems like all my energy's gone."

"Customers too," Mr. Lyman added. "Don't see half the folks come in, as just a few years ago."

"Yep. There's the faithful like Chauncey here," Kildee agreed. "And you, Mr. Lyman, but the crowd seems to be dwindling down. It's really getting to be, as the saying goes, the faithful few, with emphasis on the few."

"Well, Kildee," Chauncey replied rather bluntly. "When I was at y'all's the other night, I heard from Lula Bess that you were thinking about closing the place down."

There was a pregnant pause. Kildee didn't answer.

"Don't know what I'd do if he does," Mr. Lyman said with a sigh and almost moaned. "Sittin' all day by myself in that empty old house waiting for night to come. Don't even like to think of that. Now that the missus is gone, time sure has a way of dragging on. Especially in winter. During them cold days with the ache in my bones, you'd think spring would never get here. Winter sure does have a way of hanging on."

"Wouldn't mind having some of that winter today," the fellow from Boykin volunteered. He adjusted his ball cap, which had the logo of Levi Garrett tobacco on it and which sported in big red letters the words "SOUTHERN PRIDE."

His name was J.J. and his sidekick was Joe-Rion. They both were eating saltine crackers and tins of Vienna sausages. Like everybody else around him, they pronounced *Vienna* with a long i and e.

Kildee's back was hurting him in earnest too. He'd wrenched it the other week helping his son get a cow into a cattle truck. He agreed with Mr. Lyman that he was plumb stove up.

Still, he rose and cut J.J. and Joe-Rion each a generous slice of hoop cheese. He walked stiffly.

Mr. Lyman ventured carefully, "Better take care of yourself, Kildee and get healed. We'd hate to have to put you down like a lame horse."

He didn't answer.

Today, Kildee was wearing short pants. This was the first year he'd broken down and done it. Then with his undershirt, he presented a truly un-Kildee-like sight.

Kildee sat back down with some difficulty, put his hands on his bare knees, and carefully positioned his ailing back against the rungs of the chair.

The store was quieter than usual. Nobody ventured to start in on a tale.

Will wonders never cease! thought Chauncey, for the store was noted as yarn central around these parts and even had that reputation in places far away. That was part of its draw, for folks in the know, that is, when draw it did.

Chauncey fell to musing: *Expect folks don't have time for stories any more. They want facts and statements streamlined. Sound bytes at most. They're too busy for the meandering of our tales. Takes too long to get there, they say, like our country roads. The new times want straight roads, super highways, drawn by a ruler in city offices of men who are always on the go and no place to stay. No time to slow down and see. Got to get there as fast as you can. Folks today think they can deal with life with the same ruler-drawn line too. No walking. No detours allowed.* All this went on in his head. He didn't really have the energy today to say the words out loud.

When he'd broached the subject several days ago in this same place, Mr. Lyman had said with some astute observation growing out of his eighty-some years, "Folks want bare statement nowadays. Just the facts. Just the facts baldly stated with no humour or skill. Nothing else is efficient. People take themselves too serious these days."

"What they really want is statistics," Kildee had added. "It's come down to that."

"A sorry state of affairs," Chauncey declared. "All those sociologists and scientists, all that squirrel warren of government men. Their life-blood is statistics, such life-blood as it is."

"Straight roads and statistics," Kildee shook his head. "Yes, it's come down to that. Nine-to-five jobs and industry. Such an efficient land. They've got no use for this old store."

"Progress," Mr. Lyman said with a grunt, and with that, had had the last word.

So today Chauncey was thinking about that conversation; the silence seemed to reinforce the conclusions they'd drawn. All morning no one else had come in.

Chauncey could just hear the sociologist say, "As a social centre this place obviously leaves much to be desired. This place needs progress. We'll do a study of wretched rural conditions and make neat, tidy statistics out of their lives—for a journal article maybe."

But maybe today it's just the heat keeping folks home and making Kildee down in the dumps, and nobody spinning yarns. Chauncey put the subject out of his mind. *All we'd need is Triggerfoot as a spark to fire a powder keg of tales.*

But Trig was not able to come to the store but once in awhile. He lived a mite too far away to walk, and he had to work a heap harder on his farm, having no help or hands. "Got two hands," he'd say, "My right and my left."

The two young fellows drank their RCs. J.J. popped open another can of Viennas, and started in on another row of saltines.

Kildee shifted in his chair. His back was still hurting him some, but it had eased off a little from giving it a rest. Lula Bess had said he needed to go to bed to heal, but there he'd drawn the line. He hadn't even thought about seeing a doctor.

Again, there was silence in the store.

During this time, still no one came in. No child was at play. Not even a cat or dog was to be seen. This was unusual, but the hounds had found out cooler places on moist soil under the store or in the deepest shade. They didn't venture to move, no matter the enticement.

Kildee shooed a fly away from off his bare knee.

"Didn't ever think I'd see you in short britches, Kildee," Mr. Lyman said.

"He's trying to attract women," Chauncey added. "But all he's getting is flies. And an occasional mosquito too."

"Don't have any trouble getting women," Kildee replied.

"Doesn't take short britches for that. It's what I'd do with them when I got them that's got me confused. One's enough for me, and I learned years ago she's the right one."

"Puzzled with what to do, huh?" J.J. laughed and agreed. "I just got married last year. I'm still trying to figure that one out."

"You would," replied Joe-Rion. "At the dinner table, you're still trying to figure out the use of fork and spoon."

Fact was J.J. and Joe-Rion were eating their saltines and Viennas without either. They occasionally licked salty fingers and dried them on the camo bandanas they kept neatly folded in the back pockets of their jeans. Joe-Rion started in on a bag of boiled peanuts.

"Derned if these ain't good," he said. "Boiled just right. Salted just right."

Silence again.

Kildee hit once again at a fly. J.J. did the same.

"Get on out of here," J.J. said.

"Reckon they like Viennas, too," Joe-Rion replied.

Mr. Lyman resumed the thread he'd been upon before. "I just sure hope you don't close this store. It's about the only thing around here older than me."

"Don't worry Mr. Lyman," Chauncey comforted him. "You know he's just talking." But Chauncey took a side glance at Kildee to see if he could detect any reaction to his words.

After a pause, Chauncey continued, "What in the world would he do with himself if he didn't have this old store?

He can't farm all day, and to be shut up in the house with Lula Bess and the girls would drive him crazy."

"There's just so much fishing a man can do," Joe-Rion said.

"And real hunting season is just three months of the year," J.J. added.

"I've thought about that too," Kildee replied after a pause. He shifted his weight in the rocker, positioning his back hard against the rungs. "Guess I could make this old place into a garage and work on cars. I've done that before as a sideline when times were tough. But today the cars are mostly computer generated, and I don't have the right tools and the mind for the new machines. Trig's always said I was good with machines, that I could mount a motor on a Kleenex box, but this is another thing. And that was back in the days I had better strength in my hands to turn wrenches and I didn't mind getting up and down off dollies and sliding under cars."

"Wouldn't do much sliding now," Mr. Lyman was quick to reply. "Would more like to be creaks, jerks, and moans."

Mr. Lyman paused, then said, "Something to think of, Kildee. It's not the job for a bad back. That's one thing for sure."

"Well, you sure got a nice place here," J.J. observed, taking some peanuts out of Joe-Rion's bag. "That's all I can say. It's a good place to come and sit. Comfortable and quiet. You can be peaceful here, and hear yourself think. Nobody pestering you to do this and that. Nobody asking you to get out of the way. No telephone ringing. No cell phones. No blaring TV."

"A regular hotbed of tranquility," Chauncey this time beat Kildee to his favourite phrase.

At this description, the two young fellows would have smiled, but honoured the deadpan manner of the other men.

Now if Triggerfoot had only been there! Well . . .

Silence again, but for the regular ticking of the eight-day clock on the shelf.

"You're just down," Chauncey finally said to Kildee. "You'll spring back up with the fall when all the hunters start trooping in."

"Cool weather'll bring 'em," Mr. Lyman agreed. "Predictable as the phases of the moon, or the fall of the leaves."

Indeed, in the autumn and winter, from October to New Year's, at height of the hunting season, the old store was green with camo. It sometimes looked to Chauncey like the forest had come inside. What with the hearty greetings, hard drinking, and bluff telling of successful adventures, near misses in hunts, and the hauling in, weighing, and dressing of game, the scene would be lively again.

J.J. and Joe-Rion had in fact themselves learned about Kildee's store on one of their hunts around here.

"Maybe he's clinically depressed," Mr. Lyman said to Chauncey. "That's the words my granddaughter uses now, her and the other nurses in town."

"I'm not clinically anything," Kildee answered. "Just sad sometimes." He paused. "But never to tears. Sad just wondering if the world ain't forgot about all of us around here."

"Might be the best blessing in the world if you were forgotten," said J.J. "Try sitting your butt in a truck every day and climbing up poles so folks could watch *Everybody Loves Raymond* and *Dr. Phil* on TV."

"Or see a rotten body and blood and gore on *CSI,*" Joe-Rion agreed. "Or find out the latest on Britney Spears or who Brad Pitt's marrying this time. I'm not thirty years old yet, and sometimes I'm already fed up with the world."

"Our friend Trig Tinsley calls TV the idiot's lantern," Chauncey agreed. "A fuzzy light and a lot of noise, but that's about all. He won't stay in the room with one. 'Dangerous contamination,' he says."

"Hold on to this place, Mr. Kildee, is what I say," J.J. advised in a tone that left no room to question his conviction.

"Just needs a little livening up maybe," Chauncey looked over slyly at Kildee. He wanted to see his friend's reaction to his words.

"A few more customers is what I need," Kildee answered. "Money don't grow on trees. I still got a daughter at home and try to help out my sons and my married daughter and her husband just starting to farm. They're all trying farming in a day that doesn't want farmers; it's becoming clear to me."

By farmers, Kildee meant the real kind, as a way of life, and not agribusinessmen or the tree-farming sort who never touched the handle of a plough or put hand in the soil. All those in the store understood what he meant.

"Yep. A man's got to have at least a thousand acres now to get the respect of the world," Chauncey agreed. "It's hard to raise a family on the land nowadays. Too many bills. Not enough money coming in. If I had folks depending on me, I'd have gone belly up many moons ago."

There was a pause.

Kildee got up carefully and swatted the pestering fly. It took several tries. At last, it came to rest on Mr. Lyman's weather-worn and moth-eaten felt hat brim, which he wore year-round, hot or cold, and Kildee took deadly aim with a rolled up newspaper and not so gingerly swatted him there.

"Dammee!" Mr. Lyman exclaimed as he jerked awake and nearly fell off his chair. He'd half drowsed off to sleep and the swat so close to his ear was quite a shock.

"Got you!" Kildee declared, addressing the fly.

"And me too," Mr. Lyman answered. "Watch out how you're aiming that thing. That could give a man a heart attack."

Chauncey and the two young fellows tried not to laugh. About the heart attack, Mr. Lyman was right.

"Well, that's about the most excitement I've seen around here today," Chauncey observed.

"And the most use I've got from that newspaper in weeks," Kildee added. It was the worthless capital city newspaper, and he'd already let the subscription run out, but for some reason they were still sending it to him.

Silence again. The clock ticked on the shelf. J.J. shifted his weight in his chair. The split cane bottom creaked.

Joe-Rion got up and got him a Co-cola from the big red chest and put some change in the Luzianne coffee can. It clanked loud as it fell. He sat back down, and the sweat from the cold bottle ran down his arm and wet his rolled-up sleeve.

Mr. Lyman drowsed once again.

Chauncey's chair creaked again.

Then silence.

"Hell, if this ain't the dullest bunch of yokels I've ever seen! Me included!" declared Kildee with feigned energy.

"Who're you calling yokel?" Chauncey inquired with a fake frown.

The young fellows smiled. Joe-Rion had finished his Co-cola and sat the bottle on the floor. He reconsidered and got up and put it neatly in its rack. The clink of glass against wire was the only sound. He sat back down. The chair's split-oak bottom squeaked.

Then silence, and more silence.

"Damn," Kildee declared.

Mr. Lyman's head nodded in drowse. Even Chauncey's eyes were closed.

There were several minutes when nobody said anything, nobody moved.

J.J., a tall, handsome, black-haired fellow, was careful to pass gas quietly with as good manners as possible under the situation, but Joe-Rion was sitting closest to him and said, "Sheee-it, J.J.," under his breath, making a face and rubbing his nose.

Silence again. Several minutes passed. Chauncey now snored. His head wobbled.

"Well, if this ain't the damndest!" Kildee declared. The vociferousness of his exclamation woke up Mr. Lyman, who nearly fell off his chair once again. Chauncey snorted awake. The old tabby passing through stealthily stopped dead in her tracks, one paw raised.

J.J. and Joe-Rion looked at each other with big eyes in a kind of amaze.

"Well, this place is history! It's closed this very day!" Kildee said with dead seriousness. "Place is already dead. Just needs proper burial. The last day, sure as hell. Last will and testament of Kildee Henderson's store."

Mr. Lyman and Chauncey looked at each other curiously. They didn't know what to make of Kildee's declaration. Was he serious or not? You just couldn't say with Kildee. He might be pulling your leg, or he might be in dead earnest, uttering truth. And if the latter, you'd sure have trouble changing his mind.

Kildee's words still seemed to echo in the dark recesses of the store.

J.J.'s mouth fell open. Joe-Rion cocked his head.

"Kildee Henderson's store, rest in peace, **RIP 2007**," Kildee picked up the thread. "But from her ashes to ashes and dust to dust arises a new use for this old worn-out place. I've got it all planned!"

This time, Chauncey's jaw went slack, and Mr. Lyman's mouth, like J.J.'s fell open.

Kildee didn't give the men time to make a comment or ask a thing; he launched with zeal into his plan.

"I'm moving all the three-ring circus of stuff out of here, every jot, every dot to every i. Not a thing will stay but that old out-of-tune honky-tonk piano over there against the wall. I'll have her tuned and set her right here."

Kildee pointed to the centre of the store. "The pool table will go just here," he pointed to a central space at the store's rear. "The beer cooler will go where the farm tools had been. All those glass candy counters here in the front will be cleared out for a dance floor. And I'll make some deals with Trig for the best runs of his 'shine."

The young fellows' eyes grew large. "Is he or isn't he serious?" they wondered to themselves.

Chauncey and Mr. Lyman, who knew him well, wondered the same. They'd no better clue than the two fellows strange to the place.

"We'll just have ourselves a honky-tonk," Kildee continued. "A first-rate honky-tonk, best in the land! The jukebox will sit over there!" He signified the place that the potbellied stove now occupied. "No need for that any more. Installing central heat and air. I'll call back the vinyl-siding men."

"I can see it all now," he continued. "Crowds flocking in. Drinking plenty of beer. Dancing, playing pool. Having fun. Spending lots of cash. Lots of money to be made. Don't know why I'd not thought of it before. I'll just give the world what it wants. Simple as that."

"What kind of pool table y'all gonna buy?" J.J. inquired. "I like to play pool."

"We'll just get your suggestions," Kildee answered. "Maybe you'd like to advise. I know nothing about pool tables at all."

This talk went on quite awhile as the afternoon dwindled down, but the two fellows finally had to break off and go back to their jobs well after midafternoon. As they left, J.J. was humming his favourite current country tune. *Honky-tonk kadonkadonk*, he sang. "Hope they'll be plenty kadonkadonk," he told his friend.

Joe-Rion was driving. The REA truck engine turned over, tires sounded on gravel, and they were gone.

Chauncey and Mr. Lyman were now downright worried. Kildee was serious; they now had about come to conclude.

"A juke-joint? Hope you'll sleep on this here decision," Mr. Lyman said at last, looking at Kildee with sincerity. "I know you've got to do what's best for you and your family; but as for me, I just wouldn't fit in to a juke-joint scene. I'll sure miss this here old store."

Chauncey nodded his head in agreement but still hadn't gotten over the incongruity of a pool hall honky-tonk juke-joint dance floor on these same old well-worn and honest floorboards. He was still too stunned by the bizarreness of it all to say a word. He had to fight the vision of the floor covered in commercial carpet or linoleum.

"Well, I reckon that news got you two going!" Kildee declared. "Woke both of you up, back to life and the real world. Old Kildee's store ain't always going to be here for you. May not be tomorrow. Can't tell. Guess we'll all just have to wait and see."

Both men looked at their friend but didn't venture a

word. Too much was riding on the outcome to risk saying something damaging and glib.

"Honky-tonk or country store," Kildee said with feeling. "That's the choice of the world. We'll just have to see." He held up both hands, palm up, and made the motions of a pair of scales. One hand went up while the other went down, one down when the other went up. They came to rest even.

"But it can't be both," he said with some finality and a faraway look in his eye. "Nobody can tell what the future will bring."

Mr. Lyman's granddaughter had come to fetch him after work; and following the usual brief greetings and partings, she, who was as usual in a hurry, took him home. Annalee was a beauty, and she always turned heads. Out in the car, she had ice cream and other perishable groceries she'd just picked up from the Wal-Mart Super Store near her hospital job in town. She'd also stopped by the Dollar Store to get the rest of the little items she'd need.

Mr. Lyman walked spryly enough across the worn store threshold and was gone on his cane. When he crossed over, he wondered if it would be his last time. His step, however, did not falter. In fact, with Kildee's bad back, he almost got around better today than Kildee.

Chauncey still sat in silence, now by himself. He'd usually have paid attention to Annalee, pretty as she was, but today his mind was elsewhere.

He knew Kildee would be wanting to close up soon and get on home to supper, but Chauncey would stay just awhile longer and have some kind words for his friend. He seemed to be in real need of some.

Sure thing. Kildee wasn't himself at all today. The scales had tipped heavily to the dark side. They jolted hard that way, like when you quickly take off the balancing weight from the other end.

Same as everyone else, Kildee had his dark moments, but it was a side he'd rarely show to the world. That's what really made the day so unusually strange. It was more than just the heat.

Chauncey knew exactly what he'd do when he left the store. He'd drive right straight to Trig's and tell him what had just transpired. They'd put their heads together and decide on a course of action. This was serious business. Chauncey figured it was more than Kildee's back hurting and a slowdown in customers, and he wanted to do the best by his friend.

If anyone could, old Trig would know how to put an end to Kildee's temporary madness on these risky dog days.

They'd have to be careful though. They'd have to play this thing straight and not make Kildee mad. "Stubborn, you don't know the meaning of the word when it comes to Kildee," Lula Bess would often say. And both Chauncey and Trig knew that you needed a new definition with him. Webster's would never suffice. "Obstinate" just wouldn't do. Once he'd made up his mind, then well . . .

"Better not pick a fight during the dog days when Sirius blazes," old folks had always said. "Lessen you want one, and a humdinger at that!" Chauncey knew it was the time folks even further back called the days of madness and poetic frenzy, the time cuts and wounds wouldn't even heal. Strange days. Unexplainable things happened.

No, it wasn't the best time to aggravate Cousin Kildee. They'd best be most carefully minding their P's and Q's. Too much was riding on these particular balancing scales.

Chauncey left the store a bit shaken and with a heavy heart. He choked Blue Bessie twice before he got her in gear and could turn her front bumper toward home. He just remembered he'd have to do his milking before he went on to Trig's. He hoped Trig would be home. A serious matter indeed. All this was too much to deal with alone.

XIII

Outside the Pale

After Chauncey had done his chores and arrived at Triggerfoot's, it was what the old folks called bull-bat time of the evening, when all these little birds were circling in the summer sky on their sharp pointed wings. It was Trig's usual signal to do the milking.

Chauncey found Trig finishing his chores. After listening to the dire tale of Kildee's strange mood, Trig thought awhile and said, "You know, Chauncey, there's more to this than meets the eye. I don't know what to think. This one stumps me."

"It's got me beat too." Chauncey followed Trig through his labours in the barn.

"But give me a good night's sleep and a day to think, and I'll get to the bottom of it." Trig carried the pail of foaming milk inside. The summer cicadas sang shrill in the giant pecan trees around the old house.

Chauncey, feeling somewhat reassured, drove back up Dogwalla Road toward home. It was full dark now, and he had to keep alert for deer.

He didn't meet a single vehicle on his way. Dogwalla Road shared Kildee's description of his store as a hotbed of tranquility. No doubt it was named long ago for the fact that dogs could wallow in the road undisturbed. They'd still be able to wallow today, if the road hadn't been paved. In fact, there was one sharp turn where at least three or four old hounds would always have to get up from their sleep in the middle of the thoroughfare to let you go by. Thing that impressed strangers the most was that when the dogs moved out of the way, they moved so slow that it looked like the slow motion you'd sometimes see on TV. They were that unafraid, that unconcerned. *Why shouldn't they be?* Chauncey thought. *Folks around here had time for dogs.* They'd live and let live. What their expression looked like most was that they were truly offended that you'd disturb their peace. Not one of these dogs in the road had ever been killed, as far as Chauncey knew. The same hounds had been there for years, as inheritors of the estate. He felt it was good that somewhere in the world creatures and men could go about their lives unafraid of machines. Machines were unforgiving. They'd take a dog as soon as a man's hand or leg. You got no pity from them.

As Mr. Lyman always said, "It takes a lowdown scoundrel to run over a man's dog." These hounds were somebody's and you best not hit one of them. Chauncey always wanted to creep when he approached that curve and always had his eyes alert for dogs all along the way.

Live and let live. He'd learned to feel that way too, and that included the animals of the place, now that he hardly ever ventured far from Dogwalla Road. The faraway wide world had lost its attraction. Towns were fine to muse upon sometime, as long as they stayed far away and he could think of them from the quiet of a porch rocking chair on a summer night. *Live and let live.* He'd graduated to that.

Despite the puzzle at hand, he slept well, as was his usual way. The new morning dawned, and he went about his chores. He milked and carried in the pail. As he fixed breakfast, the sun was finally breaking through the mists. It was a new day, and maybe Trig would drop by.

As he cleared away his breakfast dishes, then skimmed the rich cream from the milk, he kept thinking of something Kildee had said yesterday morning in one of his most serious moods. "Honesty's praised every now and then, but it's always starved. Especially in these times."

Now Chauncey was beginning to piece some parts of the puzzle together; he'd at least connected a few dots.

Trig didn't stop by this day or the next, and owing to several minor calamities and emergencies at the farm, Chauncey didn't get in to Kildee's. It burned on his brain to know whether Kildee was even at the store or not, or maybe out looking for jukeboxes, beer coolers, or pool tables. The thought made him cringe.

But Trig was as good as his word. It took him several days, but at last he reckoned he'd gotten to the bottom of the thing, or at least partly so. After thinking awhile, Trig decided not to take the direct route of the straight highway. He'd not ask Kildee or Lula Bess. Instead, he went up the road a piece from Kildee's and had a good confab with the Henderson family's neighbours, the Blairs.

A Blair son had married Kildee's daughter Nolee May, and it was this young couple whom Kildee was trying to aid. She and Christopher were just getting started, and, without asking, were receiving help from both the Hendersons and Blairs. The Blairs had provided the land, so Kildee had tried to foot some of the bills for farm equipment, livestock, and tools. And then the youngsters, now living in one of the old Blair farmhouses, needed a new barn.

Of a lazy Sunday afternoon, it was to the Blair homestead that Triggerfoot hitched a ride with his neighbour, Vern Oxner, who was going that way. They drove on roads bordered by late summer wildflowers, clusters of tiny white asters, and Queen Anne's Lace. The small yellow daisies were just beginning to bloom in the ditches. It was a quiet day, and Trig felt at ease, at peace with the world.

He was on especially good terms with young Clint Blair. Clint was Chauncey's brother-in-law, and Trig knew that Chauncey had promised to look after him when Clint's sister, Chauncey's wife Hoyalene, had died from cancer back in 1984 when she was only twenty-five. Chauncey and Clint's friendship had also drawn Triggerfoot in.

Clint and Hoyalene had been very close after their mama and daddy died. They had another brother besides Christopher named Joe-Pratt, but he'd married several years ago, and was still in the process of taking over the farm. He was busy as could be.

Because the Blair land was a little too small to support another farm family, Clint went to college and became a vet. He still lived on the Blair farm with Joe-Pratt, his wife Sally, and their three children, and helped out on the farm when his veterinarian work was slow. Christopher and Nolee May lived on an adjacent farm. Chris had inherited that piece of Blair land from Grandpappy Zachariah Blair. They were hoping soon to build a new house or rework the old one they lived in now, adding on, preparing for a big family. The Blairs thus knew Trig well through Chauncey, so when he dropped in that Sunday afternoon, it was a happy occasion, like a family reunion almost.

"Wish you'd have come for Sunday dinner," Clint said. "I've been missing you and Chauncey. What kind of menace to society you been?"

"A pale poor excuse for a menace, a mouse of a menace, I'm afraid," answered Trig, shaking his head. "It's been too hot to keep up with the world."

The conversation perambulated and sashayed. It perused around curves and corners, taking its own easy time. It started and stopped, backtracked, wove, circled, interrupted itself a good many times. But old Trig knew his destination and got there precisely when it was time.

It turned out that the person who could help with information was, oddly enough, not Nolee May, Kildee's own flesh and blood, but Clint.

Seems he'd stopped by the store about a week and a half ago. While looking through his bookcase, trying to make space for a couple of books he'd just bought on a recent trip to Columbia, he ran across his sociology textbook from college. *Societies Around the World* was its name.

"Should I keep it or not?" was the question at hand. "It sure takes up room."

He flipped through its pages, remembering he'd not half read the assignments or kept up with the course but had still made a B. There were no underlinings in the textbook, and many of the pages hadn't been read. Some still were uncut, and he even had to use his penknife to open a few.

One particular chapter arrested his attention. "The Cotton South," it read. It followed a chapter entitled "The Chinese Peasant." So, having some leisure that evening, Clint sat down to read.

What he found there angered but didn't surprise him much. He remembered the reason he'd half slept through the course was its professor, Dr. J. Alfred Tudor, a much-touted expert, past middle age, a child of the sixties with a Harvard M.A. and a Columbia University Ph.D. He was wrapped in jargon and a world of statistics flying thick in a fog. His religion was progress. His dual missions were to impose his template of order on an untidy world, and to get parochial students like himself to join up with the global community and be citizens of the world. No idea of particular place or home. He'd even said once in class that his home was his job and his family his career. That's the one thing from the class Clint remembered clearly. And here Clint was a farm lad going back to the family farm. No more perfect mismatch could have been made.

For all the professor's talk of charitable oneness and the brotherhood of one world, Clint could tell his disposition was sour and he was just plain mean. "Cold" and "distant" were not the right words. It was worse. His manner didn't match his teachings or inspire confidence in his creeds. As long as the flesh and blood world could be kept far away and he could be in control of it, he loved the idea of it. For Clint, Tudor was the perfect secularised zealot Puritan from the privileged bastions of the Northeast, trying to engineer the world. He was so unlike Clint's people back home, folks with surnames starting with *Mc, Mac*, and *O'*. Clint noticed that Tudor's lips were thin and always pressed together in a permanent serious, no-funny-business way. His jaw was clenched, and he often froze it that way. *Relax. Relax.* Clint wanted to say.

Clint had made a close study of the WASP acronym. Digby Baltzell, its sociologist originator, made a case that the centralised nation should have a ruling class of wealth, the Anglo elites of the Northeast, who have historically determined and should continue to set standards for the whole. They were to be urban, filthy rich, and pro big government control. Their religion was material progress writ large, and their culture was as inherently contemptuous of Clay Bank County as it was possible to be. The white folks of Clay Bank, as Clint well knew, were from families from Ireland, Scotland, and Wales, the whipping boys to be plundered in the old land by the ancestors of folks like Tudor.

Clint came to conclude that his same professors who advanced the sociology of WASPdom were only contemptuous of his people's ancestry and cultural heritage, an existence they even felt it convenient to deny.

Sean Salyer, Clint's one good friend at school, a fellow who saw eye to eye with him on the subject, had this to say: "You know, Clint, these imperial outposts of educratic hegemony have the mission to inculcate us benighted primitives with their values. They exist so that the sons and daughters will learn to spit on their people." Sean was a brainy lad, not taken in by the scam around him. Clint was coming to see that even though he at first sounded extreme, he was right.

From the start, Clint didn't much trust Tudor and his kind's commitment to truth, but he'd give them this— they were committed to their cause. They were, in fact, overzealous that way. Clint was lost in their world, as they would have been just as lost in his. Their faith was in machines, statistics, and science and the labs and *'ologies* of men. They liked charts, templates, and grids. Clint did not. They'd adjust the surfaces and eventually create an earthly paradise. Sin was outside in conditions, and not inside the man. In the absence of God, man had to take it on himself to clean up the world. Clint saw that way of thinking as heresy of the worst kind. Chauncey had taught him what he felt about the *'ologies* and *'isms* of modern times. He was always quoting G. K. Chesterton that a new such progressive philosophy isn't really new, just an old vice repackaged and renamed, but vice just the same.

Clint mused: Sociology 102—the new secularised WASP religion of the land, stemming straight from the Age of

Enlightenment, which he and Chauncey always laughed and called the Age of Endarkenment. Of an earlier age which the modern elite deemed "Dark," Chauncey had passed along to Clint a passage he'd found in his Chesterton—words to the effect that if the Dark Ages were dark, it was only the church that brought them out of it. *'Ologies* and social engineering had no part in that progress at all. He and Chauncey had been reading C. S. Lewis. Clint looked up at a small card on which he'd hand-lettered a quote Chauncey had given him from *The Pilgrim's Regress*:

It is the same with all their machines. Their labour-saving devices multiply drudgery; their aphrodisiacs make them impotent; their amusements bore them; their rapid production of food leaves them half starving, and their devices for saving time have banished leisure from their country.

Clint turned his eyes back to "The Cotton South." As he read, he saw now exactly why he'd usually opted for much-needed sleep when it came time for preparing next day's class.

There was one section of the chapter that was entitled "Are Southerners Really Lazy?" Its conclusion was *yes, but don't blame them too much; it's their environment and heredity that's the cause. Down there, it's too hot to work, and the legacy of slavery made men who sat on porches sipping juleps and wasting their lives.*

Clint flipped to the textbook's title page. He should have known, *New York, Henry Holt Publisher, copyright 1953*—New York, capital of WASPdom, the Kingdom of

Thingdom, the land of abstractionists, globalists, progress, banks, CEOs, industry, the elite, the filthy rich. Indeed, Clint felt this book to be a product of the post-World War II progressive generation—when everything had to be plastic, polyester, aluminum, Bauhaus glass and steel, and above all lock-step new. That's the time when Clay Bank's store buildings on Main Street all lost their honest old-timey individualised façades of brick and stone and were covered up with sheaths of precast, prepainted aluminum or flat stuccoed over to make a blank featureless face, like all the other ones being done across the land. Clint called the look "plasticized." One size fits all. Or, better, make them all fit into the one single mould. It was the secularised crusading Puritan triumphant. How cost-effective efficient! It was the new faith. Everything intersected at right angles and fit so neat. Round holes for round pegs. Clint figured he, Chauncey, and Trig were square pegs and never would be rounded down.

"The greatest generation. What bull. The most destructive, most selfish, and the greatest egos," Clint muttered to his wall. He'd come to believe that the United States had also lost the war. They'd destroyed the country themselves without one enemy's bomb. Paving everything over into the Parking Lot Nation, trying to make everything slick, shiny, and new. He knew his farming South had lost that war big time. But what else was new? As the stories told by his people impressed upon him, that same slaughter had been going on now for nearly 140 years, or really maybe

700 if you thought about his people way back in old Ireland. Cromwell's Puritans. They'd followed his people over here too and had invaded and burned them out once again.

Progress, progress, and more progress, the chant of the century. "Progress Our Most Important Product," had said G. E. "Better Living Through Chemistry," DuPont had proclaimed. Chauncey had told him that these were the Apostles' and Nicene Creeds of the new religion of the land, the religion of money, founded by men in the great power centres of the Northeast, filthy rich with power and controlling the world. To them, progress really only meant more money, no matter what else was lost in the grabbing. Yes, "more money," the word "progress" finally boiled down to that.

He remembered Clay Bank's own motto when he was going to elementary school. *ADVANCING CLAY BANK* it read, with an arrow behind the big red words on a billboard going in to town. The local chamber of commerce had also printed the slogans for plates for the front of your car.

The arrow on the billboard had always looked threatening to him, pointed as it was in the direction of his family's farm. Now, he could see that it was an arrow aimed at him.

Even as a young fellow, he wondered, "What would the fiery-coloured arrow do if it hit our big barn?" The question would run through his mind when he looked at the billboard from the seat of the school bus. And sometimes he would see their barn in flames with cows and horses kicking frantically to get out. His family would all be carrying buckets of water, but the buckets spilled, or the water boiled out dry in the tin pails before it could be used on the flames.

Clint read further in "The Cotton South," his mind passing from mildly curious to absorbed. The various authors of the chapter were noted Southern progressives. He knew enough history to be able to tell. Howard Odum, Hodding Carter—he'd learned something of these men. They were not his kind, more like the enemy and thus easy tools of the holders of power.

The expert chosen from the nineteenth century was Frederick Law Olmsted, an abolitionist whose works were designed to be persuasions for his cause. He painted a picture of wretched Southern farms. The academic note introducing his description of his travels in the 1850s showed the same old twisting Clint had been accustomed to in history classes. It told how keen and trustworthy an observer Olmsted was, so you'd believe his words. The note ended with informing you he designed New York's Central Park. Too bad it didn't also show how the island with its hills and springs and creeks was flattened to make a grid pattern of right angles for easy and efficient real estate sales.

But what was left out was Olmsted's biases, and the fact that he might have a major axe to grind. Such an introduction was not meant for balance in getting at the truth. Clint felt it was nice to know the author designed Central Park, but for the matter at hand and in the interest of truth and honesty, it would have been more pertinent to note the ideologies that may have coloured Olmsted's views. The textbook seemed to be doing the same in its biases. Clint shook his head.

The business with Olmsted was but one example Clint found. If he were a scholar, he'd been able, no doubt, to find many more. Lord knows what others there were. At any rate, this was the sort of thing that fed him up with college in his six-year sentence there.

Clint read on late into the night. One essay in the textbook attacked porches on houses as backward, bad places because people sat there talking too much about the past. If they only had air conditioning and a TV like city folks did, then they'd be able to connect to the world.

"Yes, the sleazy world of Jerry Springer, *The Young and the Restless,* and the *Maury Povich Show,*" Clint said out loud. He felt that somebody needed to call to reckoning the men who made bucks from lowering the cultural norm in such a foul way. The popular scene often appeared to him to be no better than an open sewage flow.

Or if not watching TV, these new modern folks would maybe be at some college studying what a negative influence porches are. A nice scam. Maybe in the right classes they'd learn to be hustlers, men like these textbook authors, and would thus make big salaries for doing nothing, and be able to survive without farm sweat in an every-man-out-for-himself, cost-effective, profit-and-loss, nine-to-five world. Or maybe they'd get a job in research in the new Raptor jet aircraft factory and make better, more efficient weapons to kill more unfortunate people around the world in forcing them into the template of their own unhappy land. Clint concluded: *These WASPs are just new and improved Cromwells in disguise. I'm glad our people hailed from the hold-out Irish county of Waterford.*

Yes, the backward old farming South. It was all the porch's fault. He reckoned that's why all the houses in these Clay Bank subdivisions built in the 1960s and '70s, like in every other city and town sprawled across the continent, were constructed in precisely the same so-called "ranch" style, a long one-storey, ruler-drawn, hermetically sealed affair—no porches anywhere to be seen. And nothing close to a ranch about it. Same old twisted double speak, saying the opposite of what you mean, the lie to hide the lack. When a society doesn't respect language and say what it means and mean what it says, Clint's favourite writer had declared, it's preparing its own doom. Not standing by words was the best sign of a people's doom.

He guessed the "ranch" was some kind of postwar, efficient, progressive urban style decreed by those in a cold land (cold in more ways than one), where you froze most of the year and never ventured much outside. When you did, he reckoned you had to move fast lest you freeze in place. And the car could come inside with its enclosed double garage bigger than any other room in the house. You'd not have to press soil to get in the car, and the automatic garage door opener made muscles obsolete. The houses looked to him for all the world like thick low brick walls, segments of the Great Wall of China strung out on the landscape, stockadelike, to keep out nature and the world. Or maybe they formed the paling against life. He remembered how the invaders of Ireland created a fortress pale about Dublin, and outside this radius, the unregulated, unruly native people lived. The regulators, the imperial masters of the land, held up inside their shining stockade city on a hill. Chauncey had told him that's the way we got the expressions "outside the pale" and "beyond the pale" to mean the unspeakable, ungoverned, and indecent, the uncivilised. "The disorderly and untidy world of outer dark," Chauncey had said.

But porches mean neighbourliness, Clint protested to himself. *Friendliness, hospitality.* Oh, but then that would be just another one of those quaint, old-fashioned porch fictions from the past—all right if it's just pictured as a thing out of history in a movie or in nostalgic Mayberry reruns on the black and white screen.

Clint was proud of his people. He thought how good it was that the old Blair farmhouse, like all the others in his community, had porches, front and rear. The houses were designed to face east-west, so the sun in the summer would not be striking one of the porches at any given time of the day, giving you a cool place to sit; or in winter, when you wanted the sun, it would touch one porch in the morning, the other in the afternoon, and you could sit with the sun on your face.

Hereabouts, the porches were used. Its where his family most often gathered to talk, relax, solve problems, share sorrows and joys, entertain neighbours, sing and play fiddle, look out at a palingless world, and beyond, at the stars and moon. To him, it was a friendly, social place, a gathering centre, the frequenting of which was as important a ritual as sitting down at the big pine table at meals. They'd even invented a verb for the practice. "Let's go porch," his sister Hoyalene use to say.

Clint had noticed on his drives to and from the university that on some of these old ranch-style houses along the way, a new generation of owners were now building on porches to the ruler-drawn fronts. He concluded, however, that it sadly must just be a fashion thing because he never saw anyone sitting on them, not even kids. The obligatory newly painted rocking chairs were always empty next to big expensive potted ferns. Fast lifestyles and A.C. and computers still enticed the occupants away. It must have been a kind of nostalgia that was putting them there, something lacking in their lives and a vague understanding that something was, a desire to fix something that had gone terribly wrong or supply something that was missing, yet which in their minds couldn't be quite pinpointed. Or maybe the porches were talismans like guard dogs or sphinxes or griffons to keep evil away. Cerberus maybe? Some shape to fill a lack? He just didn't know.

But Clint felt that at least it was a hopeful sign that the nostalgia of porches somehow still lingered there. It had not been completely erased by the learned pages of *Societies Around the World*.

Clint read on. Now another author lamented there were no good restaurants in a rural land. Maybe, Clint thought, that was because everybody knew how to cook and did.

Maybe they had the time and good healthy home-raised makings for meals and liked to be at table with their families and friends. The food was fresher and you knew where it came from and where the hands that prepared it had been.

Then his eyes fell upon the page of illustrations for "The Cotton South." They shocked him the most. At top was a huge industrial complex complete with iron-scaffolded towers, monster aluminum drums, pipes breathing out vapours, a smoke stack pumping a cloud to the sky that blotted out the sun. There was a squirrel warren of metal conduit pipes and tubes, all at crazy angles tangled into themselves. It was a minotaur's labyrinth of angular metal like none the ancient Greek could have conceived, not even in its most imaginative phase. To Clint's mind, it was the very image of hell. He surmised that only Dante could have envisioned the scene.

Clint read the picture's caption: *Part of the installation at Decatur, Alabama, for the manufacture of Acrilan, one of the new synthetic fibers.* Yes, a miracle synthetic fibre plant in the chapter on the cotton South, his cotton South, and the touting of synthetic, plastic, and aluminum progress. It didn't take long to get the book's drift. In the South, "*in the chemical industries, development has been particularly rapid,*" the caption concluded. And that was supposed to be for the good. Progress here in a word meant industry.

Acrilan. The word sounded like some utopian land, some futuristic fantasy city somewhere over the rainbow, some new Oz or Never-Never Land. Or, better, maybe it was some new synthetic Camelot made of miracle plastic where perfect people walked about on the perfectly lined golden cloud streets wearing shining clothes woven of shimmering miracle thread. All the streets intersected at right angles. The ground was unblemished flat. The land of Acrilan would be enclosed in a glass dome, fully climate controlled. Rain would only fall with the turn of a dial. That is, if any rain was permitted to fall. It would stay one perfect temperature all the year round. Everything inside would bow to man's will. Outside the dome's pale was the uncivilised, the untidy unpaved, the ungovernable, the dark that had not bowed to man's light and will. The dark and its mystery were threats and above all to be feared.

Then as contrast to the Acrilan towers, at the bottom half of the illustration page was the porch of an unpainted country store. The store signs read *OLD GOLD, COCA-COLA, CASHEL'S, ROLLING ROCK, MURTAGH O'BRIEN'S GROCERY.* Clint had left Kildee's store just this morning, and had seen the same signs. The photo reminded him fondly of home. The look of it had the same salutary effect upon him as the magic words "the old home place." Both were anchors in an unsettled world of flux.

In the doorway of this store stood a tall fellow, no doubt Murtagh O'Brien himself, looking for all the world like Kildee. He had on khaki pants and a short-sleeved cotton shirt. He was propped with one arm high up on the doorsill, and looking casually out on the gallery where sat five men in straight chairs and rockers. One had on overalls, the others khakis and jeans. Their light-coloured shirts contrasted with their skin. All five had on hats or caps of one kind or another. One man was drinking an RC. Another had a cigarette in his mouth, slanted down. They were rocking or propped back at leisure, conversing among themselves, passing the time of day. No doubt, they constituted some of the essay's lazy Southerners.

Three worn wooden steps led up to the wooden porch, just like at Kildee's. The porch and its people looked welcoming to all. There was no screen on the door. It stood wide open, as it always did at Kildee's.

The front porch's tin roof had column posts of cedar trunks, with the heavy knots and stubs where the limbs had been, still protruding from them. The posts hadn't been shaved, hadn't been smoothed. It looked all so natural to Clint. Out of nature, the posts were, not from the planers and mills of men. Coming from this rooted place. Nothing like them at Home Depot or Lowe's, or any other such warehouse on wheels. They were used as supports, not as pointed palings aimed at the breasts of men to keep the enemy life at bay. Murtagh O'Brien most certainly lived outside the pale.

Yes, for all the world, the store in the photo was just like Kildee's. It was a comfortable, comforting scene. Clint was at home there, as with the Acrilan plant, he'd felt foreign and strange. In that top photo he'd sensed the same threat he'd experienced as a lad at viewing the arrow on the *Advancing Clay Bank* billboard pointed at his loved ones and home. Now in his newly formed understanding that pointed arrow linked up with others to create the invading enemy's weaponry.

Clint kept coming back to the illustration of the porch of O'Brien's Store. He looked at it long and mused, imagining himself there. If he were in the picture, the men could easily be his friends. He'd like to know that fellow on the left, with the ball cap, who looked about his age, the one with his cane-bottomed chair leaning back against the store wall and with his white cotton shirt sleeves rolled up and the first buttons open at his throat. Clint liked the independent way he sat his chair.

The old gentleman in overalls reminded him of his grandpa. He sat with feet planted firmly in front of him, his hands on his knees, facing matter-of-factly the cameraman. Not much could ruffle the calm confidence of this man. He'd seen a lot, suffered a lot, and was still there.

From Mr. O'Brien there in the door, Clint was sure he'd be able to learn what he'd need to know of the community and could get at least a few rattling good tales. He imagined sitting at his potbellied stove in winter and him spinning yarns.

Knowing the textbook's theme, Clint had steeled himself not to be too surprised at the caption for this photo. Unlike praise for the new magic synthetic fibre chemical plant in a geography of nowhere, the country store received the sociologist's damnation complete.

Below: the country store. The store serves as one of the few meeting

places for the Negroes of the community. As a social center it obviously leaves much to be desired. It represents the wretched conditions under which a large part of the people of the South pass their lives.

Clint sat there for a few minutes stunned. Even though he'd prepared himself and shouldn't have been amazed, he still was. After awhile, he shook his head.

And this is what our schools teach us. To be contemptuous of our people and spit on them. A bitter smile flitted across his lips, his eyes showed hurt. *Sean Salyer was right. No wonder the world calls us hayseeds here in the flyover country. Colleges teach it. And no wonder I felt lost in that place. So all-fired sure of themselves, in their tidy worlds.*

Clint felt it was adding insult to injury for the system to have impoverished the land of its farming communities and then to look down upon them for being poor. It was like stealing silver spoons from a family, as Clint knew had happened all around here in 1865, and then criticising the robbed one's table for not being set in high style. Grandpa Blair had told him the story of Sherman's bummers he'd had from his own grandpa. They'd stolen all the Blair silver, the livestock and food, then smashed and burned what they couldn't steal.

Clint wondered how one of those six people in the human-scaled photo of the store would look when transposed to one of the huge metal-scaffolded towers of the Acrilan plant. You'd not even see him, he'd be so small. But the man would certainly know he was there, even if unseen—there breathing the chemical vapours spouting from the tubes and pipes all around. Every day—eight to five, and often overtime—breathing the toxic air. The tubes reminded Clint of those hooked to patients in hospital rooms. He could only see a very sick world laid out strapped on a table, anaesthetised, or in a coma; but instead of the tubes carrying life, they were pumping chemical death instead, keeping the patient lying there, preventing his recovery and health.

Maybe that same fellow on the tower would forget where he was standing for a split-second and fall. There were great open vats of steaming chemicals below. Hydrochloric or sulfuric acid, no doubt, or newly created poisons whose names he'd never heard, mile-long words that no one could pronounce or remember, all the products of the Progress labs, the seeming fantastic creations of mad scientists in a world gone mad for money, ease, and the latest fads, the engines that ran this land of Acrilan, where smoking bonfires of fuel lit the scene. Yes, hazard upon hazard. He hoped the fellow on the left in his white shirt hadn't gone to work there, or changed his comfortable cotton fibres for the mesh of Acrilan, a mesh like an entangling net or a spider's web.

It was now well after midnight. Clint went to bed. He told Trig and those assembled there at the Blair house that he lay on the verge of sleep playing a game of checkers on the picture's store porch. His congenial partner was the old man in overalls who reminded him of his grandpa. In his mind, this man taught him wise lessons from his treasure of anecdotes. "Crown your king," the old gentleman kept reminding him, in punctuation of his tales.

Clint said he heard the old man say quite distinctly, "You

know, young feller, it's natural for a person who thinks of himself as a beast to act like a beast. Then the next logical step is for him to let people treat him like one." Clint said he'd drifted into sleep seeing men turned to animals, some pitifully gazing through the chain-links of zoolike pens, topped with razor wire, some grazing on all fours like sheep inside electrified fences, or cattle prodded along and corralled into place in assembly slaughter lines. His last waking thoughts that night had been of birds caught in entangling nets and snares, or others dead at the bottom of wire cages hanging high among the smoking towers of Acrilan.

XIV
More Lessons Learned

After Nolee May served the two men on the porch tall glasses of tea this lazy summer Sunday afternoon, Clint resumed his narrative. Trig was still listening intently, for once saying few words. He rocked at ease, taking the story in. So absorbed was he in Clint's telling that he didn't notice the sweat from the tea glass dripping on his pants legs. He made no comment to Nolee May that the tea was just like he liked it—so sweet it hurt your teeth.

Clint reported that a few days after he'd burned the midnight oil studying his sociology text, he'd taken the book over to show Kildee.

Yes, Clint had definitely decided to keep this volume in his meagre collection despite limited space in his bookcase. It had turned out to be worth a lot, but not in the way its authors designed. Instead, it was a perfect example of what he'd been telling folks about the contempt the world from which he'd just come held for them, the world from which he'd newly graduated and gotten his homecoming degree, as he put it, thank the good Lord. He hoped he'd escaped with the minimum of damage done.

The folks at home had never really half-believed the things he told. What he'd said had sounded too far-fetched, too illogical, too unreal, making no sense at all. Surely, nobody could be as foolish as Clint was saying they were. They felt he was just exaggerating, although, as they admitted, the levelheaded Blairs usually weren't given to that trait very much. Now he had proof.

Kildee had not been too lively this past week. What with a strained back and much on his mind, his spirits were about as slow as his walk. Because there weren't any customers, he and Clint had uninterrupted time.

So Clint had shown Kildee the book.

When he'd looked at the page of illustrations that pictured the country store, he didn't say a word. Clint kept silent too, watching the muscles in his friend's jaw clinch and grind.

When Kildee got to the store caption, his cheek twitched.

"Well, that's what I've been telling y'all," said Clint.

"Guess they've got to take the hard-earned taxes we pay, to set up schools to poke fun at us, hold us up as folks living what passes for lives." Kildee had gotten the words of the caption down correct. "To use our money to poison the minds of our own young. That's just not honest or fair."

"Honest and fair, Mr. Kildee? Words like that aren't much thought of today, except as high-sounding covers for scams, or for skullduggery to hide behind. Like plastic fibres, it's a synthetic world. Nothing natural or true. Things done on paper in triplicate, with statistics, abstracted life lived in the mind on forms, jobs and careers as homes, words as games, cause as faith, agenda as creed. *Synthetic*'s the word. And oh how civilised. All of us folks here are just outside the pale."

"Civilised? Old folks always used to say that civilisation took a great tumble when open fireplaces were given up. That's one reason why Lula Bess and I still use them today. But not the rest of the world. Now I know what they were getting at. It gathers us all together around the hearth, makes us love the simple dooryard things, as Uncle Dick says."

After a pause, Kildee continued. "Well, Clint, now at least you got a license to doctor on cows, cats, and pigs, as the professors in this book doctors on men. Did you ever feel like a lab rat while you were over there?"

"Most always," Clint smiled a pained smile.

"When I'd tell old Trig my problems with school, he'd always reply, 'They's just shooting themselves in the foot. They'd be shooting themselves in the brain if they had one.' Trig's a smart one, cuts through most all kinds of crap. Of all the ones I talked to, he was the only one to follow me straight off and believe. He and Chauncey, that is, but Chauncey had reason to understand. He'd been there before."

There was another pause, and Kildee's eyes looked down. He didn't want to meet the eyes of his young friend. In some ways, he felt he'd failed him in this—in not listening better, in giving Clint the appearance of not believing him.

"Thanks for bringing this in," he told Clint at last, handing the book back to him. "I've been trying to think here of late about the paths I'll be needing to take. I'll factor this here photo in. Seems as one of the benighted primitives, as you say they call us, I've got some hard lessons to learn and some even harder choices to make."

Clint didn't know exactly what to make of that, and didn't have time to ask because Kildee launched in, in a way that showed he was much more aware of the times than Clint would have believed. Each was learning more about the other, and both liked what they saw, even if it had been learned out of pain.

Kildee thought for awhile and chose his words well: "It's been more than fifty years since these photos were taken and all these claims made. *Acrilan.* I think I had an Acrilan shirt many years ago when I was a young married man. Yes. Acrilan and Ban-Lon. For a while, they were the rage. Lula Bess bought me what they called a knit Ban-Lon shirt. In summer, it felt like wearing a plastic bag. Which, of course, it was. I remember I sweated my ass off first day I wore it outside in the sun. Miracle fibre? Miracle was it didn't kill me with dehydration. Well, I conveniently 'lost' that shirt real soon, I tell you. Never wore it one more time. Lula Bess kept asking, 'Dee, dear, where's your new miracle shirt?' But she never could find it. I cut it up to make tomato tie strings. It worked right well that way, and that's the only way. It wouldn't even make a decent rag, wouldn't soak up water at all."

Clint laughed, "Like wearing a plastic bag, huh?"

"Yep," Kildee replied. "Cotton for me and none of these miracle fabrics."

"Same here," Clint agreed. "Young folks are seeing that too. The old Progress World War II generation is them that's most likely to want plastic things—from plastic clothes to plastic flowers in the graveyard. Lot of us young folks think we've got in danger of having nothing but a plastic world. Everything virtual or by proxy or on a screen."

After another pause, Kildee ventured. "I reckon the miracle's worn off. Now, wouldn't it be a good college study to go to Decatur, Alabama, and look up that Acrilan plant. Wonder if it's still there. You can see it was planted right down in what must have been a nice big rich field. In the far distance, you can still see rows of what looks like corn. Wonder what that countryside looks like now. Wonder if it ain't paved or poisoned to death. I don't think they make Acrilan anymore. If they do, it's probably made in Mexico."

"Or China, more like," Clint corrected him.

"Yes, and wonder what ghost town it left if the plant did leave. Some statistics-loving professor type should show us the statistics on the PCBs in the ground. Or what the river the plant dumped in now looks like downstream. Wonder how many folks got cancer drinking that water or smelling the fumes. Nothing synthetic or abstract about cancer. That is, if you got it. Now, compiling the statistics should show about that. Where are the college folk with forms and calculators and interviews scouring the place and poring over records? We've had half a century since your book came out with all its promises and predictions suggesting what us poor primitives should do in leaving our farms for factories and towns. Maybe your prof needed a new textbook that would update the progress and look at today's real scene. See if those predictions came true and the promises were made good."

"Yessir. You're right, Mr. Kildee. With all those eager-to-be Ph.D.s in the Ph.D. assembly line—looks like one truth-seeking, honest, bright professor could encourage one bright, honest young mind to follow up such a lead. But the Progress and Science grant-getting cult still has a hold on that place and all over the land. The corporate types and their set of government grant givers still have the power. The industrial-banking set still calls all the shots from their perches of power. They use smoke and mirrors to perform Yankee peddler tricks and miracles. That's what they're paid their big salaries to do. But it's the same old Yankee peddler tricks. Synthetic means *new made by man to fool you into believing it's better than the genuine thing, which of course it cant even come close to.* More than like, it's just cheaper and easier to make because a lot of machines are involved and people are cut out of the process."

Kildee had said, "Sounds to me they act like they want to play God and substitute their world for the one He made."

"Yep," Clint continued. "Now cloning and genetic engineering's all the rage. Folks on farms, like you and me, Mr. Kildee, we're the ones to be done away with, with their disappearing act tricks. We're God-fearing free natural men in nature. That's the real problem with us. Chauncey says he believes they want men to be synthetic too, all abstract and hollow, like ghosts. Easily regulated and standardised by their managers, easily fooled and persuaded, moved around like chess pieces on a board to pick up and go where the jobs and promotions are. The regulators come from a geography of nowhere and want nothing to do with you and me. God created us, not man, and we come from a place. So that reflects poorly on them, and they want us gone. We're proof of their scam."

"Well, the old store in that bottom picture," Kildee had said after awhile. "Didn't pretend to be what it wasn't. Awful as they claim it was, it didn't kill people with chemical vapours or give them cancer, or poison their air and their food and rivers. Didn't leave behind PCBs and wrecked dreams."

"You're right, Mr. Kildee, and it kept things to a right and proper scale. The world stayed natural and not synthetic man-made. Folks dealt with folks face to face. And the store stayed put and could be counted on to be there when you needed it. It didn't pick up and run to China because a little more profit margin could be made with a low-wage scale." He'd taken up his book and prepared to go on his way.

Kildee knew the rightness of what Clint had said, but the textbook had put him out of sorts. Folks noticed that and said he was in a foul mood all week.

That day, to several customers, he'd said mysteriously out of the blue, "Well, that's just the last straw."

Clint finished his narration there on the porch. Triggerfoot had continued to listen intently to every word. Nolee May brought them refills of tea.

Then Clint went to his room and brought out the textbook to show Trig the picture Kildee had seen. He passed the book around.

"Looks like a happy enough bunch sitting there at the store," Clint's brother Joe-Pratt observed. He'd joined them out on the porch. His wife Sally came out with their smallest child. So did Nolee May. All gathered to look at the picture, heads in a circle, gazing at the page. Then passing it around, they each had time for closer scrutiny. Now Sally rocked gently to and fro once again, getting back to the peacefulness of her usual way. The little boy half slept sitting on the porch floor with his back and head against his mother's leg.

"Them men's all talking and being friendly, seems to me," Triggerfoot said. "Probably telling stories, laughing, talking about the crops, the weather, passing the news. And taking their time. Stories reminding of stories and with a lot of curves and detours. Look at that little fellow playing with the Walker hound under the porch. Dog looks like my old Bleat. Sure could be his twin."

"I don't see a dog in the picture," Joe-Pratt said.

"But you know one's there," Trig replied. "It's just too dark under there to see. Look deep. He's the spittin' image of Bleat." It was Trig's rich imagination at work once again. Folks knew him and understood his kind of truth that was, on balance, a little truer than the unvarnished fact.

"The store sure reminds me of Pa's," Nolee May agreed. "Nothing plastic there. No plastic storefront. No simulated wood-grained walls on the inside. No vinyl siding on the outside. No plastic shirts. No plastic chairs." There was a long pause.

"No plastic men either," Trig volunteered. Another pause.

"Nothing synthetic there," Sally said.

The day had dwindled down, and Vern stopped to fetch him home. After a courteous while, saying at least three times that they had to go, the two finally took their leave. They declined Sally's invitation to supper, both having chores to do at home.

As they were leaving, Joe-Pratt picked up his Granddaddy Blair's fiddle tucked on a window ledge behind a shutter on the porch, and began to play. It was an old fiddle tune learned from his pa. Trig, who also played and sang the old-time music, recognised it at once as "Sweet Prospect," one of Singin' Billy Walker's shape-note tunes from his *Southern Harmony*. Singin' Billy was born in these same hills not too far away, near two centuries ago. He'd learned many of the tunes at his mother's knee as a lad. She was a Jackson from Ireland and brought the old music with her to the new land. As long ago as that was, Trig still knew Singin' Billy as one of their own. As Kildee was often heard to say, "Folks around these parts have long memories," and Trig proved it true.

Triggerfoot hated sorely to leave. If he'd been on his own, he'd have stayed, chores or no. He'd no doubt added his own voice to the harmony. But he'd gotten part of the answer for which he'd come. Mission accomplished. A college textbook had lit a fuse to the dynamite that now had power to rock several worlds. The fuse was burning; and unbeknownst to Clint, he himself had been the one to light it, and at just the wrong time. The fuse was still burning on. They'd have to see if anyone or anything could put it out in time before real damage was done.

As they started carefully down the Blairs' dirt road, Trig could hear the Billy Walker tune loud and clear, played in earnest now, ringing down the furroughs and fields. Joe-Pratt was known as a very fine fiddler here in these parts where he wasn't the only one, and talent like his wasn't scarce. He was much in demand at socials around.

Sweet fields arrayed in living green, the old song ran, *and rivers of delight.* Trig knew every word. It was a perfect end for this part of his day.

The Blair meadows bordering the road were brim full of Queen Anne's Lace nodding full heads over the rich green, and to Trig, the sight seemed to be exactly what the words of the song said. The pits in the road made them drive so slow Trig had the time to notice a tiger swallowtail on a blue aster, drinking his fill.

"Here's to old Singin' Billy," Trig finally said to his friend. "His music still sings after so many a year. God rest his soul kindly for enriching our own." On the way home, Trig hummed the tune and occasionally broke into song with his rich baritone.

Vern was impressed. He'd heard that Trig had a good voice, but he'd never realised he could sing like that, and with such feeling that way. The treat and surprise of it there in the truck, he'd probably be remembering and speaking of for years. To have such talent so close and not know!

He and Trig from that day on would be better friends. He'd see to that. And he vowed he'd not overlook the worth in other ways, of things at his door, a lesson Trig already knew.

"Vern," Trig said as they pulled into the lane that led to his house. "Seems to me, the lesson of that-there book is that some place is better than just anywhere. I know it ain't the lesson the book meant, but it's the lesson for me." After a pause he continued, "Chauncey just the other day was saying that the world out there sometimes calls us around here the barefooted provincials. He'd been thinking that them among us who's always admiring their shoes are the real provincials, whereas me, Triggerfoot, he says I'm parochial because I'm not concerned with whether I'm shod or not, or what kind of shoes they are. He says that them who fear they're provincial, are provincial. I don't wait to hear what the world out there has to say to trust what my eyes see. He said he was paying me a real compliment, and it took me awhile of riddling, but I think I finally understood exactly what he meant."

There was a long pause in the conversation at that.

As the truck came to a halt at Trig's door, Vern looked at his passenger. "Trig, it was sure a real pleasure having you along for the ride," he said.

"Much obliged," Trig answered, and his back was silhouetted against the bright as he opened the truck door. He slanted his hat toward the setting sun as his tall frame ambled toward his barn.

XV

Passing the Test

Next day, Chauncey showed up at Trig's door. He'd just been up to Kildee's store and found nobody there. As always, it wasn't locked. But when Chauncey walked in, the room was empty and silent as a tomb. The light on its cord, which always burned when Kildee was in, today wasn't on. The empty dark weighed heavily. Chauncey glanced around uneasily and quickly left.

He drove straight to Trig's, where he found his friend out chopping wood.

"Well, Trig," Chauncey said in his usual way, hiding his unsettled state.

"Well, Chauncey," came the reply.

Triggerfoot was mean with an ax. Although now past his prime, he was still stronger than any of the young men around, and could outlast them in such strenuous chores. His frame was lean and looked its strength.

For Chauncey, there was even a lesson here—as in just about everything his friend did. He watched as Trig balanced the last sticks of stove wood he'd split this morning. No neater woodpile was ever stacked.

"Trig, you build that thing better than most of the expensive houses in that new Plantation Acres subdivision on the edge of town, not to mention the ones called Green Acres, Tall Oaks, Cedar Creek, and Tanglewood."

"Ain't those places a hoot," Trig replied. "Green Acres ain't green any more. It's mainly sidewalks and asphalt. Tall Oaks don't have any oaks, tall or small. In Cedar Creek, there ain't a cedar left, and with all that washing from bulldozing, the creek has silted up and disappeared. What little was left was put in pipes under the ground. So in Cedar Creek, no cedar, no creek. In that fancy Tanglewood, ain't no woods left to tangle. They cut 'em all down to build three-car-garage homes with swimming pools. Of course, you can't have leaves blowing in those fancy pools. Plantation Acres hasn't seen planting in years. Wouldn't know what to do with a mule, not even a John Deere, except for those little green riding lawn mowers they use to make a grass desert out of their yards."

"Mow-and-blow yards, I call them," Chauncey added.

"Not even a rabbit or bird can find a place to hide in them deserts, not to mention food. No cover for a living thing in mow-and-blow yards. But Plantation Acres, it's still called."

Yes, Chauncey thought, *in a synthetic world, words no longer attached faithfully and honestly to things*. In the usual way, it all smacked faintly of scam, his chief word for the times. Hype and marketing were the new kings of the day. All this boosterism was little better than huckstering, the modern snake oil sales, with the emphasis on snake, a world in which you'd never mean what you say, and people wanting it that way. *Humans nowadays*, Chauncey thought, *are the only species on the planet that beg to be lied to and misled.* Maybe the truth around them was just too hard to bear. Maybe the scam believed was the only way to face what they'd made of the world. Yet Chauncey knew that the lying, and willful believing of the lies, just took them farther and farther away from the way it was intended to be. He wondered who'd break this fatal chain. He knew it would have to be somebody from outside the pale but had no one in sight.

As to why he stacked his woodpile with such precision, Trig replied, "Well, three things Pa always said tells the character of a household—how straight the rows are ploughed and how neat and high the woodpile is stacked in the fall."

Trig paused until Chauncey predictably asked what the third was.

"How soon the slop jar gets taken out in the morning."

As much as he usually enjoyed Trig's meanderings, today Chauncey came straight to the point. "I've got bad news. Kildee's not at the store."

"Do tell," Triggerfoot answered. "I'd been surprised if he was. But about all that, I too have got some news. I need a breather; let's go porch for a spell." Trig took his undershirt from the nail on the shed and put it on.

Like the Blairs, Triggerfoot used *porch* as a verb. Chauncey had picked up the habit too. "This thing's got me worried," Chauncey declared.

"Well, I'll tell you what I know. Might put you at ease."

As they walked to the farmhouse, Chauncey asked, "You reckon Kildee's out looking for pool tables and jukeboxes?"

Triggerfoot laughed. "Not likely," he said.

"Well, where else could he be? His truck wasn't at home. No sign of anyone around."

"Yep. Got us worried, ain't he! But I got the inside on that. Nolee May said that they'd gone up to Flat Rock to see Lula Bess's first cousin and aunt."

"When did this happen? How long they been gone?"

"Since yesterday morning early, and will stay up there about two weeks to give them a break. Kildee's sons and Nolee May and her husband are doing his farm chores."

"Well, that's at least some kind of relief. Thanks, Trig."

"No problem."

"Reckon I better get back on home. Cows to be milked, wood to be chopped same as you. Much obliged for the news."

"Yep. No problem," replied his friend once again. "I've had me a breather. Now I can tackle that wood with some built up steam. Glad you come."

Despite his declaration that he had to get home, Chauncey lingered awhile. The talk was light and bantering, and genial above all.

"Don't be a stranger, Trig," declared Chauncey, looking back at his friend as he finally made his move. "Come up Dogwalla Road some time when you can and stop in for a meal. I'm usually there."

"When you ain't at Kildee's store, you mean."

Blue Bessie pointed her tarnished and pitted front bumper homeward. As he drove, Chauncey saw Trig once again at his work. As his friend faded from sight, Chauncey thought back over their conversation. Trig had briefly alluded to Clint and Kildee's textbook episode. Chauncey didn't doubt the effect it would have had on either Clint or Kildee. He let his mind wrap around the scene and gave his imagination full play.

He recalled what the tortured recluse Franz Kafka had said about books; they were the axes that split the frozen sea within. He and Clint had talked about that some months ago and had come to the conclusion that they had to be the right books and that too many of the wrong ones could freeze even a warm sea instead of making axes to free a frozen one.

These past few nights in his reading time before sleep, Chauncey had been in a Gaelic phase. In one of his forays into that world, he'd discovered the verse of one Eoghan Rua Ó Súilleabháin. From the dark days of the ancient culture's eclipse, Ó Súilleabháin lamented the death of the bardic way of learning. Chauncey read how the bards were the university profs, the *ollamh*, of their day, the much revered ones, rightly venerated as those who, besides being the keepers of the people's knowledge and wisdom, had an intimate record of particular places and their meaning. Their truths were based on place and never derived from the written word. Chauncey struggled with his Gaelic. *Faoin dulraidh*, he said aloud, slowly, tentatively, striving to get the pronunciation halfway right. He enjoyed hearing the sound of the words over the motor's clank and hum. At home when he said them in the quiet of his alcove, they had a magic sound, like some chant from a holy man.

Faoin dulraidh, he repeated as he looked out over the passing lonely fields and patches of deep wood. The *faoin dulraidh*, as Chauncey had learned, was a special category of bardic lore—songs in praise of place, the tales and traditions attached to holy hills and particular ancient trees, or rivers, or wells. It was a chief duty of the bard to sing them. He taught these to his students, and passed them over the land, enriching and protecting the tribal memory, strengthening the people's identity. Chauncey reckoned this must have had the salutary effect of making the folks value these places more and thus protect them from the worst abuse.

What you know well, you're more likely to love, and what you love, you won't abuse, he'd reasoned. It was a simple equation, so simple a truth the driven world of utility and progress wouldn't want to get spread around. It wouldn't be good for business at all. He'd talked this over with Clint just the other day.

Chauncey knew this same feeling for particular sacred spots, rooted as he was. The word *homeplace* had a magic sound, the talisman to ward off the evils of the day, and Clint knew it too. Chauncey was aware that his tutelage had deepened what was already there. Kildee had known the passion as well, and, yes, so did Trig, especially Trig, and so unselfconsciously. This was also the case with the Hendersons, Simses, Jacksons, Eisons and Eppeses; the Glenns, McMorries, Douglasses, and Blairs; the

Rogerses, Connellys, and Kellys; the Perkinses, Gordons, Lyleses, and Grahams—all the family connection there. It was a knowledge bred in the bone and in the collective blood and imbibed through a mother's milk. It must also have been that way to the ancient Gaels, but the bard strengthened and applauded the vision and way. A man was one with his land. There was at that golden time no inside and outside the pale.

Chauncey continued to let his mind wander in these well-worn paths as he slowly maneuvered the weave of turns and curves going home, one hand on the wheel and his left out the window to feel the air, greet it, and only stopping to wave at the few he met on his way, in fields or on front porches, or at the wheel of the solitary car. *Faoin dulraidh* and Eoghan Rua Ó Súilleabháin, the way of learning of old. To be taught without books on the fertile land, to be able to recite for hours the grandest poetry of highest wisdom, place, spirit, and memory, praise and commemoration—learning it in the dark and deep of night, in total darkness with not even a guttering candle allowed, when the spiritual world hurried near and there was no distraction of superficial light and sight. Yes. The university of old. *Faoin dulraidh*. Mere pages were secondary to chanting the world.

Another ancient word came to mind. *Duchas.*

"*Duchas* and still *duchas*," he said aloud. The chanted sound was like another spell against the ailing times. *Duchas*, the old love of the local engendered through stories tied to a particular place. *Duchas*, he said again, *duchas*, relishing the feeling of its slow syllables in his mouth and on his tongue, the sound of it against the murmur of tires against pavement and the truck's muffled roar. It was like his own best scuppernong wine in whose taste he could detect his own soil. Like the water of his well from its granite bedrock, that taste was his alone and signified home. Like *duchas*, like *faoin dulraidh*.

Then the words of Ó Súilleabháin came back to him out of his reading last night, elegiac and grieving, tragic, and gut-wrenchingly sad. The poet was lamenting the supplanting of the old holy knowledge imparted by the bards in the current day of invasion and loss: *There were lost besides honour and nobility, generosity and great deeds, hospitality and kindliness, courtesy and noble birth, culture and activity, strength and courage, valour and steadfastness, the authority and sovereignty of the Gael to the end of time.* An elegy for a lost life.

Chauncey quoted him aloud from memory: *Loss of learning brought darkness, weakness and woe on me and mine. Amid these unrighteous hordes, oafs have entered the place of the poets, and taken the light of the school from everyone.* It was an invaded Ireland, and full three centuries ago, but Chauncey felt that the poet's words described precisely his own beleaguered place and time, and the displaced remnants of these same families invaded and dispossessed in the old land.

He and Clint had talked about this too. Chauncey had introduced him to Ó Súilleabháin, and Clint understood from the start. What the university did today in sending their products off to live where the job was, was the polar opposite of the mission of old. Abstraction and suspect *'ologies* now replaced tying down through the realities of spirit and earth. He and Clint had come to seeing the world in the same way.

One of the brightest lights in Chauncey's life was his friendship with his brother-in-law. It had become more than obeying his wife's last wish that he see Clint through. He'd fostered Clint as she'd wanted, out of duty, out of promise, but he also had genuine affection for him. Chauncey could see that Clint's mind now moved in paths very much like his own.

Indeed, the old inspired and holy bards, the *ollamh* of their golden day, they spoke to him, and now their echoed collective voice from long ago, in the words of another Gael, a long drawn out death song of an order, monstrous in its intensity like a dog howling after its departed master—the curse of the poet, fatal always, upon a jaded and decadent time in love with death and approaching its end. It was the curse of the poet on the invader, the enemy, the dispossessor of the genuine good and true.

Chauncey was glad to come out of his dark reverie into the light. Up ahead, he recognised Spurgeon Adams's truck coming his way. It was easy to spot because it had more cab than bed, unlike the great majority of the trucks around the community.

He and Adams stopped in the road and visited through their open truck windows. Spurgeon had just been by Kildee's too and found he was closed. He'd then driven straight over to Mr. Lyman's and found the old gentleman sitting alone on his porch. Spurgeon waked him from drowse.

Adams figured that since Mr. Lyman went to Kildee's store every day with his granddaughter, Kildee wouldn't have left Mr. Lyman without warning he'd not be there, wouldn't have made Annalee drive him back home.

Mr. Lyman had told Adams the same news that Trig had gotten from Nolee May. He was in Flat Rock with Lula Bess and would be back in two weeks.

Chauncey wondered why he hadn't thought to go over to Mr. Lyman's. He should have known Kildee would have filled Mr. Lyman in, but he reckoned he'd panicked, and first thing he usually thought of in a tight was Trig.

After more than a ten-minute chat there in the road, Chauncey could see a car coming toward them, cresting a hill behind Spurgeon. So the men broke off and went on their way.

Chauncey drove on automatic pilot. His mind was elsewhere. The cool breeze coming from the woods and fields, he didn't even feel or credit this time, as he usually always did. On his final mile home, it came to him in a flash just what to do. It was a moment of inspiration that came to his hungry mind like manna from the sky.

The scheme flashed all at once fully developed, all of a piece. Chauncey smiled, and knew that this would do the job, if anything could. After they got through with this, Kildee would just have to keep the store open. Of this, Chauncey felt sure. But they'd have to hurry to accomplish this thing. No time to waste.

So instead of pulling onto his dirt road leading home, he veered left and drove up to Nolee May's.

XVI
Store Raising

Nolee May was peeling apples on the porch for a couple of pies when Chauncey arrived. The red peels curled around her white hands. Chris had picked them yesterday evening from the trees his grandmother had planted on the hill behind the old farmhouse. As he gathered them, he had the feeling that the kind old woman was helping him fill the pail. The same trees had yielded the same pies now for three generations of Blair wives.

"Why, Chauncey," she said. "That's great. I like your plan. What can I do?"

They talked action. Chauncey admired Nolee May. Like her father, she was always the first to pitch in. Cooperation not competition was her byword. Chris could be counted on as well.

Chauncey got excited about the little projects she said she'd engage in, to fit into the overall plan. A few of these efforts weren't so little at all. But starting this early, she'd have almost two weeks and could do them in her off time from housework and chores.

"It's the least I can do for Pa. He's been so good helping Chris and me, getting us started here on the farm."

On that day and the next, Chauncey went over to visit Kildee's three sons on their farms and made half a dozen more house calls. These folks in turn were supposed to get in touch with more. It was like a phone tree or an e-mail list, but face to face.

Everybody was happy to pitch in. They'd start right away, and in two days—this Saturday—they'd come together at Kildee's store. That would give them plenty time before Kildee and Lula Bess got home. All the folks who came around to Kildee's and valued the place and their friend promised to help.

As Triggerfoot had always said of the people in these parts, "You can count on a promise. If somebody says he'll be there at ten, you can bet he'll be there at ten. If a man says he'll help you, he will. If a man says he'll kill you, better start packing to get out of town. They do what they say—and call it by the right name. They call dung dung and not angel food cake. These were other ways Pa said you could tell what a man's made of. He had little to do with them who weren't honest with words. Lyin's worse than stealin, he'd say."

So on Saturday morning bright and early, the work began. Those who said they'd be there, were, and at the time they said they would.

First thing Chauncey did was replace the rotten bottom step of the trio that led to the front porch. He had Joe-Pratt plane him a thick piece of cedar. He'd measured and precut it the day before. It fit like a charm.

Mr. Lyman's agile teenage grandson climbed up on the roof of the rear shed porch and fixed the leak in the tin. He then started in with his push lawn mower and sling, attacking the weeds and tall grass behind the store. As he cut, he took off his shirt to get him some sun and, truth to tell, show off a little before the girls. He had a good build.

Mr. Lyman's oldest granddaughter's husband replaced the half-dozen porch floorboards with old heart pine. The boards matched in a neat fit. Chauncey helped him.

Kildee's eldest son Lyles, whom they nicknamed Kildee Jr. because he looked so much like his father, brought in the display cabinet he and his brother Glenn built from some salvaged eighteen-inch-wide walnut boards. It was a beauty of a job. The two installed it in a place Chauncey knew Kildee'd approve. They stocked it with the boxes of cigars and shotgun shells Kildee had had to put in a jumble on the floor out of the way. This improved the place in a number of ways. First and foremost, you'd not be tripping over them anymore.

Kildee Jr. and Glenn surveyed their work with deserved satisfaction, standing together, tall and straight like Kildee.

Susan and Polly, the daughters-in-law—Lyles' and Glenn's wives—polished the glass candy counters that were sadly smudged by the hands and noses of the little ones. They'd promised to come back next week to sweep up and do more. Susan had three well-mannered young Henderson children who played about the store and more or less stayed out of folks' way. Polly had two, with one more on the way.

Kildee's middle son Barham (they called him Bannie)

and Bannie's pretty auburn-haired wife and children had the Henderson farmhouse detail. They were to make a few repairs. They showed up with food for dinner and to give moral support to the working crew.

Nolee May brought in the first two pairs of thick chair cushions for the rockers that sat by the stove. They were covered in cheerful red-checked cotton, and fit perfectly the backs and seats. She'd have time before Kildee returned to do the six more she'd planned. Various workers sampled the cushions from time to time. Susan and Polly said they liked them so much they planned to use the pattern to make new cushions for their own rockers at home.

And Nolee May spread the newly made bright flowered cotton tablecloth over the table in the corner of the store. This is where her pa ate sometimes at midday. The pattern reminded her of a garden in spring.

She made a mental note to have fresh cut flowers there in a vase the day he got back home.

Spurgeon Adams brought in his new purchase—a fine oscillating fan. There were plenty hot days left in the year.

Adams also made plans with Kildee's sons and Clint to chop up some wood. By next Saturday, they'd have delivered and stacked up enough stove wood in the shed room at the rear to do about half of the winter. If they got some more help, they'd do more. They'd like to have enough for the year, Bannie and Glenn declared. So they'd see.

That afternoon Chauncey set to work painting the privy

walls inside and out while Mr. Lyman's grandson climbed on its tin roof and painted it a bright red.

Mr. Lyman wound Kildee's granddaddy Lyles' eight-day clock, then went out on the porch and sat down. He enjoyed to the fullest watching all the activity without and within. He'd not seen so many people at once in the store since he didn't know when. He thought to himself that the sight would have surely done Kildee good.

About noon, the assembled broke for dinner. They sat around where they could, their food on their knees. Nolee May, Susan, Polly, and Billie had brought fried chicken, big fresh-baked biscuits, potato salad, cheese pie, a coconut pie, and a beautiful large whipped-cream pound cake with white icing. They got drinks from the cooler and put their coins in the can. They all had a jolly great time telling tales, swapping news, enjoying each other's company. One of the sons said, looking around him, "Didn't know work could be so much fun and could taste so good."

The clock ticked from its shelf. During the day, several other store regulars drifted in and out and contributed this work and that. One brought a new trashcan to replace Kildee's near bottomless old beat up drum. Another set to work replacing the rotted or fallen palings in Kildee's fence. He promised to come back next Saturday, weather permitting, and give it a new coat of paint.

Triggerfoot came in about noon with Bob Graham, who'd been in to town. He stopped by for Trig. After joining in the dinner, they both set their broad backs to work splitting up the wood that Kildee already had there.

Bob also brought Kildee a much-desired treat, a quarter truckload of coal. Kildee never allowed himself such a luxury. Bob brought with it a shiny new tin coal scuttle with poker and tongs he'd picked up at the hardware store. Triggerfoot contributed a brass spittoon that was stored in his barn. He set it by the potbellied stove.

Trig said with satisfaction, "Now some of them no-mannered guests won't have the excuse to spit on the stove anymore. I know they like to see and hear it sizzle, but that's just one of life's little pleasures they'll have to do without." Some of the women thanked Trig and heartily agreed.

In one of his pauses from wood splitting, Trig declared to several men in hearing distance, "Looks like a barn raising, but instead of a barn, it's a store."

Chauncey heard this from inside and said to Mr. Lyman's granddaughter, Annalee, who was tidying shelves, "I reckon I've been raised myself in this store. And if that's the case, then I reckon I'm a store raising too."

Annalee's brown eyes smiled.

She sure is one pretty woman! Chauncey thought. Oh, to be twenty again.

Chauncey knew there was much truth in his declaration of how he'd been educated. He came to Henderson's store pretty empty of anything compared to the knowledge of people and place he now had. He could honestly say he knew far more about human nature today, the good and the ill. True, he was degreed when he got there, and had a lot of better-than-the-usual book learning, but now this was a different know. His other kind of knowing had made him more or less passive to the world. The fuller his mind had got, the less active he'd become. And his training had been to keep the world at a safe arm's length.

He'd learned much since then, especially about the little dooryard things, and from all the folks around. So he'd give back to this place now, like alumni of colleges give to their schools. It was only right that he should. It was, after all, both his starting and finishing school. Like Clint, he'd also gotten his homecoming degree.

About two o'clock, who'd show up but J.J. and Joe-Rion! They'd gotten their curiosities up to see what had transpired since the day they'd left. After being filled in on the news, they straightway took off their shirts to keep them clean, and pitched in helping Trig and Bob chop and split up the wood. It gave Trig a much-needed spell, for he'd been laying it on, doing about twice as much chopping as Bob. He had chopping down to an art.

J.J. and Joe-Rion said they'd come back during the week and put in that new electric outlet Kildee'd been vowing to do for years.

As the sun made its progress down the sky, clouds were gathering in the west. They augured a summer downpour. The folks made preparation to leave. It was about five. Trig went off with Bob Graham in Bob's big new Ford truck, heading for home. Trig bantered with Graham that he'd always wanted to ride in a tank. He said he liked the big oversize truck bed and that Bob hadn't got one of those extended-cab models. It had become fashionable for everybody in town to buy trucks, and the big comfortable cab is what they wanted. Trig called them sissy trucks.

Chauncey was the last out the door, he and the resident stray dog that had adopted the place as his home.

Kildee had made provision with Clint to keep the dog's bowl full. Clint checked, and it was—full up to the brim.

Clint was another, like Trig and Kildee, you could most especially count on. So were all the Blairs, Grahams, Lyleses, and Hendersons too. Chauncey knew he was richly blessed in his friends.

His marriage to Hoyalene Blair had opened the door to a new world. Now if only she could be there with him. He touched through his shirt for a moment the little gold locket that held her picture. He'd worn it now for some twenty-three years. It seemed so short a time since she died. His father had died of cancer like her only a few years before Hoyalene, and he remembered how at that time, he felt so alone in the world.

Before he turned home, he drove up to the old Blair family cemetery and stood silent for a while at Hoyalene's grave.

The crooked crosses, granite roses, carved wreaths, and marble urns made his head spin in their jumble with carved hands pointing upwards, little lambs for the dead children, plain fieldstones of the pioneer graves shining with mica, the pink and black polished granite of the new stones. Each had a story to tell. The thought dizzied him with too much life he'd never know and that couldn't come back again. He thought he'd better leave. Here his mind did not rest or find the comfort some found.

He thought of Hoyalene. She had only to stand in an orchard or field and put her hand on a little apple or peach tree, or a cornstalk coming into tassel there, to make you feel the goodness of planting, of sowing, and tending, and, with luck, a full harvest at last. All her strength of will to live came out in that gentle touch, a rich mine of life, far dearer than gold. She had faithfully kept the farmer's covenant. And now she was gone, so suddenly gone.

He touched the locket again. She had been taken from him, and for a while, his own life was gone with her too. Now the wound from the rending still bled. He was like a tree split in two by a lightening bolt. At times like this, he knew she was there with him but not saying a word. He listened but to no avail.

Annalee's brown eyes came to mind. They were so much like Hoyalene's. His last thoughts as he shut the heavy cast-iron gate were the same ones he'd had in the store. The gate clanged.

"If I were only half my age!" he said to the dark summer clouds now upon him. They promised a rain that would finally break the heat of the dog days. As he opened the truck door, a few heavy cold drops struck his skin. They stung. He looked through a rain-spattered window at the heavy grey stones of the cemetery wall. It was made of big blocks of stacked granite, held together by the heft of them and no concrete, a wall as solid and heavy as grief.

He drove home slowly in the bursts of rain, thinking

about the teamwork he'd organised today and the pleasure it had given them all. He'd never done anything quite like that before and it felt good. Necessity and loss had taught him a lesson he should've known long before.

At times today, he'd paused and looked around at the faces of his neighbours and friends as they chattered and bent to their chores. He liked seeing them there and that he was a part. Now out of his recollection, the one image that stayed longest was Annalee's beautiful, simple gesture of freeing a fallen dark lock from across her face with a sweep of her hand and, at other times, the way she'd use her lower lip to blow strands into place. She reminded him so much of Hoyalene and embodied so much of what was good in the place. Here the good was holding on, lasting into a new generation.

He steered the truck carefully into his rutted drive, listening to the splash of his tires. The rain had slacked off. For the first time today, he felt tired. It would be a comfort to sit down on his own porch in this cool and fresh-washed new world gleaming with wet, once his farm chores were done.

XVII
The Centre Holds

The following Saturday was another clear summer day. It was the first weekend in September, and very early this morning, those raised on the land could detect just the slightest hint of fall in the air. It gave their steps extra spring. Soon the leaves would start to turn in what Chauncey's mother had called the amber days. Already a few yellow leaves from the giant walnut behind Kildee's store whirled down when a breeze riffled through them.

As predicted, the good rain a week ago had broken the heat of the dog days. All the week had gotten a little cooler with each day that passed. Most of the farmers around had even sowed their mustard and turnip greens. The days were noticeably shorter now.

Kildee and Lula Bess were still at Aunt Bessie Caldwell's in Flat Rock, so Chauncey and his friends had plenty of time to carry out their scheme at the store.

But today Chauncey was not the first on the scene. Getting there at seven o'clock, he thought he would be, but when he drove up, there were Trig and Bob Graham unloading wood.

"Well, Chauncey," Trig said, waving a gloved hand.

"Well, Trig," Chauncey replied as he set in to unloading a new cushioned high stool for Kildee to sit at behind his counter. The old one had been repaired so many times that raw nails snagged your pants, sometimes your skin, and despite all the attempts at fixing, it was still shakey in the extreme. Chauncey often wondered why Kildee hadn't hit the floor.

"That's shore a good idea, Chauncey."

"Kildee's butt will appreciate this red-letter day at least," Graham nodded at Trig.

Chauncey went in with the chair. He stopped to wind the old eight-day clock on the clock shelf. Its tick tocks sounded merrily, just as Chauncey had heard so many times before. Today the pendulum seemed to swing eagerly, with determination.

"While you're at it, Chaunts," Trig said from the porch. "Take a look at that clock dial. Seven o'clock. Were you going to sleep all day?"

Then Goldie Oxner came up with Mattie Lou DeWalt in Mattie's little grey Toyota truck. The two ladies were first cousins, neighbours, and close friends. They'd made up a cheese pie, fried a chicken, fixed a coconut cake and potato salad, and brought two jars of tea. They had their heads tied up in bright red rags.

The two would help mop, sweep, and get all the spider

webs down off the store's rafters. They also brought a big stack of funeral-home fans.

"These no-count men can use them on the porch to swat flies away," Mattie Lou said. Men, she knew, didn't often use fans. It would take some doing to get them to. But in this, as in most things, Goldie declared, the women could lead the way.

The front of the fans had images of Jesus in Gethsemane, or as the Good Shepherd with his shepherd's crook and holding variously a lamp or a lamb. There were rural scenes of country churches in fall. Funeral home advertisements embellished the backs. Mattie Lou put them in the little walnut cabinet made by Kildee's Grandpa Lyles that sat at the store's front door. It was he who'd built and begun the store.

"At least the women folk can get some use out of them," Goldie grunted. "If the men are too lazy or proud."

The two ladies were stout and the floorboards creaked under their weight. They bustled about.

About nine o'clock, Bo Peep McMorries drove up in his pickup. He fetched in a big plate of barbecued pork and ribs covered with tin foil. The meat was soaked in the mustard-based barbecue sauce they all liked. After turning them over to Chauncey, he set to work with Trig. His wife Merle joined the ladies cleaning counters and dusting shelves.

Then in came the Blair family contingent, Nolee May bringing the rest of the rocker cushions she'd made during the week, and Chris laden with carpentry tools to complete some much-needed repairs. He'd be helped in this by his older brother Joe-Pratt.

Clint bore on his shoulder a new bag of dog food for the resident hounds. He was in especially good spirits today and joked as usual with Graham and Trig. With this break in the heat, folks had been calling on him more often to doctor their farm animals and pets.

"Miss Goldie," Clint said. "When I rode by your yard this morning and saw all that fresh wash on the lines, I knew all was right with the world."

"Yes, suh, Mr. Clint, I'm doing fine. Looks like you are too," she replied. He had more than the usual red in his cheek and a brighter than usual sparkle in his eye.

There were clothes on the line most sunny days in Goldie's yard. She had a big family to wash for, and sometimes did washing for white folks in town. The neighbours all said that when they saw clothes on her line, they knew all round these parts was well. Somehow, it gave needed comfort to those who passed by, like monuments and landmarks in towns.

"Shore is looking fine, Mr. Clint," Goldie added. "You've grown into a good-looking boy. Your mama and pa would be proud."

"Regular babe magnet, I'll vow," Mattie Lou added and said, "Uumh-uumh. Bet the young ladies see it too." She looked in the direction of one particular young beauty, Ida Alston, who was helping Nolee May polishing the chairs. Ida acted like she didn't hear but blushed a little and hid the traces of a smile.

All the folks who'd promised to come today did. J.J. and Joe-Rion got there in the morning this time and had put in a second electrical outlet before noon. They'd put the first one in on their work break two days before. Today, they got there extra early. They weren't about to miss the midday feast, for feast they rightly knew it would be.

Spurgeon Adams brought in nearly a cord of wood. It still had to be split to go in the stove, but Bob, Trig, and Clint would make short order of that job.

Kildee's three sons helped the neighbour put the second coat of paint on the fence, taking pains not to get more of it on Lula Bess's hollyhocks, four o'clocks, and sunflowers. They'd finished the job by ten.

Their wives had brought in several kinds of cakes, fried chicken, fried rabbit, and various covered dishes of vegetables. With Mattie Lou's and Goldie's brimming full plates, they had to set up two extra tables to make room at Kildee's own.

They were followed by Danny and Beebo Thomas, successful farmers from down near Triggerfoot's home. They'd raised a hog, and yesterday morning they'd killed and butchered it. Last night, they slow-cooked it. For the last eighteen hours, the two brothers with the help of a friend had taken turns sleeping, telling tales, minding the pig, and having nips from the communal jug. Now they bore warm pans of brown succulent pork, potato salad, a coconut pie, and a peach cobbler made by their wives. They and Trig were good friends. Beebo went back to his truck, and this time had his hands full of carpenters' tools. He farmed for a living but made extra money doing small building jobs.

Folks around knew he did good work. Danny had a grass sling. He set in to finish cutting the weeds around the store and across the road.

At about ten o'clock, Danny and Beebo's Aunt Verta May Suber drove up with more food. She had a big bowl of black-eyed peas she'd raised herself with the help of Beebo and Trig. She went back to the car and brought in a pot of rice in one hand and a bowl of green beans in the other. She'd picked the beans just yesterday off the neat tepees of half runners she and Danny had planted in her pa's old garden back in May. She'd cooked tender pods of okra on top of the beans the way the Subers and most of the folks in the neighbourhood liked them.

Verta May was accompanied by Mr. Biddie Sims. He was a deacon of Verta May's Weeping Mary A.M.E. Church and a friend of the Blairs. Everyone knew that Biddie, a widower, was sweet on Verta May. He brought several folding chairs.

At about 10:30, Mattie Lou's husband Eison drove in with Goldie's husband Dan and their oldest son, Jeter. The three carried hammers and saws and set in to work with Beebo and Kildee's sons making repairs on the store's loose or broken clapboards. Eison and Dan were strong and skilled and made the work fly along. Jeter was still learning but could hold his own.

"Seven is better than four," Eison declared, and with that, Kildee Jr., wiping sweat from his forehead, was the first to agree.

Yesterday, Kildee Jr. and his brother Glenn had helped

Spurgeon Adams deliver the wood they'd promised to get there today. They did it early, so they'd free up this morning for more work. And this had worked out well. With all the help, they finished by noon, much earlier than they'd figured they would.

The morning was soon gone in a hubbub of activity. By dinnertime, the folks had the place looking ship-shape. All told, there were forty-nine people at the store to eat dinner. It looked like a family reunion or church dinner on the grounds.

As folks were gathering around to get ready to help their plates, Nolee May said, surveying the scene, "I declare. Pa will be so proud. He won't recognise the store."

"Yep," added Kildee Jr. "All the things he'd been saying he wanted to do, and put off, over and over again, usually 'cause he was helping us instead, we've done. This'll make his life easier. Sure appreciate all y'all folks' help."

"Shows how much Pa's appreciated around here," Glenn added.

"Seems all of us today are like a big family," said Bannie. "Thank y'all for being here."

Mr. Lyman and Annalee hadn't been able to make it to the store till twelve. He grumbled that he'd been ready by six and sat waiting, but Annalee had had some emergencies. Still, they'd got there for the rest of the day to pitch in as they could. Annalee brought in a big chocolate layer cake, baked sweet potatoes with the dark sugar oozing out of their brown jackets, and a heaping split oak basket of biscuits. She'd made the cake yesterday, but it was the biscuits that was one of the emergencies. She'd burned the first pan. Mr. Lyman always considered what he called black bottom biscuits a family tradition, but these had black middles too, he said.

So at one o'clock, they had all been gathered in, and picked up the glasses and plates Nolee May had made sure were there. They stood by waiting for everyone to get on equal footing, talking and joking, visiting, sharing the news. Coming in the door with rolled-up sleeves, Trig could be heard singing in his rich baritone, words of his own making set to the tune of "Just a Closer Walk With Thee." The new lyrics ran "Just a bowl of butter beans. Pass the biscuits if you please. I don't want no English peas, just a bowl of butter beans." At last, Chauncey quieted them all down.

"Folks," he began. "Friends, neighbours, family, thank y'all for being here. Mr. Lyman will grace our food the Lord and kind ladies have provided us." He looked at Annalee.

But Mr. Lyman, whom Chauncey had brought up front, and who'd been ready to say grace, wasn't saying. Chauncey looked at him with another nod as signal to begin.

Instead, there Mr. Lyman stood with his mouth open and frozen still. He was in the best position to see, facing out as he was, as everyone else was facing in, the tall, familiar figure in silhouette at the door. It paused, looked around, and entered.

Mr. Lyman, though his eyesight sometimes played tricks on him, was dead right this time. He couldn't believe it, but sure as the seasons come each after each, it was Kildee. He and Lula Bess had returned a few days early. As they told folks later, as much as they enjoyed visiting Aunt Bessie and Cousin Dana, they couldn't wait to get home. For them, as for most of the folks of their neighbourhood, travel went back to the French root of the word *travail*.

Chauncey was the next to see, and his face turned a little red. Those assembled, figuring that these two men saw something behind them, turned around. From the looks of these two, they wouldn't have been surprised to see a grizzly bear.

Then such clamor of greeting, hugs, and laughter could never have been imagined by anyone the day before.

Well, suffice it to say, Kildee was just about floored. When he first drove up and saw all the vehicles around the store, recognising most, but some of them unknown, he'd said to Lula Bess, "Somebody's died." But that didn't seem right either. They'd not come to the store. "Or maybe somebody's drowned and folks are parking here to drag the river."

No possible solution to the mystery could either entertain. Then he stepped on the first, the bottom step, to the store. It was new cedar and the second and third didn't give. At a glance, he saw the new painted palings, and in the distance, the privy's shining red roof tin. The split wood was still scattered at the store's right. One stack was building to the rear. All of this came instantaneously in a blue blur. It was a little too much to take in.

For a minute, he wondered if he'd sold the store before they left and forgotten he did. Or was this store his? Did they get the right place?

Then his eye caught the hand-painted green and white canvas

banner over the door: *WELCOME HOME DEE AND BESS.*

"Well damn if we ain't surprised the surprise party," he said to his wife.

For weeks, he'd tell the story over and over again, blow by blow, moment by moment, coming in. He never tired of telling the tale and of his reactions, each and every one, spreading his words like a feast before hungry listeners. He changed the story a little each time. The embroidering was more elaborate than his wife's silk on linen scenes. His usual wry humour was the salt and pepper to grace the meal.

Oh, yes, grace the meal.

So Mr. Lyman was about to try again, and he was even more eager because now they'd even more to be thankful for. Lula Bess and Kildee were back home safely with them, or "where they belonged," as he put it.

Kildee's sons and daughters, their husbands and wives and children gathered Kildee round. Then the neighbours and kinfolk, close and distant, circled around that gathering.

Chauncey quieted the group once again, and Mr. Lyman who was poised, opened his mouth for the blessing's first word.

But interrupting, Kildee proclaimed, "So, I reckon this is what's meant to be in the bosom of family and friends. No better bosom for me! I was plumb lost in Flat Rock these past two weeks. I'm glad to be home."

The crowd assured him and Lula Bess with another full round of laughter, applause, hugs, handshakes, tears, slaps on the back, a kiss or two, and a few cheers.

Poor Mr. Lyman. He'd try once again.

This time he was successful in blessing the food. He kept it brief, knowing what the situation called for.

"Father. We come before you today, a blessed people gathered here." His eyes were shut and his head down. The only other sound was the tick of Grandpappy Henderson's clock.

"Thank you for the gift of life and for this place. Thank you for him who keeps it. Bless him and his own. Thank you for neighbours, family, and friends, and for this food. Amen."

In his excitement over Kildee's coming in, and his thanks that Kildee had come home safely to them, he'd almost forgotten to put food in the list of things to be thankful for. A few laughed at that. They gave Mr. Lyman proper tribute as patriarch of the place. He was the oldest in the community now that Mr. Joe-Blair Graham and old Mr. Caleb Lyles had died.

During the hubbub preceding grace, Kildee had had a chance to ask Goldie and Verta May who was responsible for all this.

"Mr. Chauncey," Goldie replied. "It was sho' him."

As folks helped their plates, Chauncey had a chance to greet Kildee.

"Well, Kildee," he said.

"Well, Chauncey," Kildee returned. The two men went to shake hands, but it was Kildee who refused, instead putting his outstretched right arm over Chauncey's left shoulder in an embrace. In all the years, it was a first.

"I needed that," Chauncey said.

"Me too."

No more was said. Folks crowded around. The food, needless to say, was superb as always, and done proper honour to, by plates mounded up like the hills in these parts, or maybe more accurately, the mountains at Flat Rock. Groups gathered in threes, fours, and fives, sitting when they could, scattered around from the store, to the porch, and the yard.

Though Kildee and Lula Bess had had nearly a three-hour drive from Flat Rock and had lighted for the first time there at the store, they weren't really tired. All this excitement had made the adrenalin run.

After dinner, Kildee tried out the newly painted privy. In the quiet there alone, he had time to marvel at the paint job on its walls and all that had transpired in the store while he was gone.

"Mr. Kildee's in there," he heard someone outside say. "Wish I had a firecracker or cherry bomb." Another laughed at the thought of such a juvenile prank, then silence again, and Kildee went back to his thoughts.

It took Kildee some time to see all the improvements that were wrought the two short weeks he was away.

"Each day's like Christmas," he declared to Trig, a week hence. "I keep finding things all y'all have brought in and done. Y'all must have been hustling to do all y'all did in such a short time."

Trig and Chauncey could tell a great change had come over their friend. It was more than the fact that his back problem had cleared. Even the tone of his voice had changed.

Trig commented to Chauncey that it was like a dark shadow'd been lifted off of him.

XVIII
Hospitality

"The main traffic of life is, after all, with one's own spirit. If it be gentle and affectionate, how can the journey be aught but joyous?"
—Archibald Rutledge

It took awhile for Chauncey to learn the details of Kildee's two-week sojourn with Lula Bess's mama's people away up in Flat Rock. Although these particular family members had moved away when they married, Lula Bess was still close to them. She was, in fact, named for her Aunt Bessie Oxner Caldwell, with whom they'd visited.

Aunt Bessie was her mama Kat Oxner Blair's baby sister, and Cousin Dana was her mama's brother's only child. Bessie was thus Cousin Dana's Aunt Bessie, too, and more like a mother than aunt.

Kildee and Lula Bess told Chauncey they truly enjoyed the change in scenery, and not having to follow any routine at all each day. That is, they enjoyed it at first, but after awhile, they started to miss home, especially at night. They even missed the routine.

It wasn't because their situation wasn't pleasant. The mountains were cooler. The old house was breezy, comfortable, and spacious. Lula Bess's aunt and cousin were good gentle companions, hospitable as the day was long.

"Aunt Bessie, I think you've got to be the most hospitable, generous person I've ever visited with," Kildee claimed. "What's your secret? I sometimes don't have near the patience you do."

"Well, Dee, thank you," she said after thinking awhile. "But our circumstances are different. You run a store. I don't see folks every day, like you. I don't get many visitors, and when I do, they're extra special, a real treat. You see folks constantly, over and over, every day."

"But it's more than that, Aunt Bessie. I can't put a finger on it though."

They were sitting in old high-back rockers on Bessie's front porch looking southward over her neatly clipped lawn at the distant hills in the direction of the misty blue-green of Kildee's home.

"I learned this bit of wisdom from my mama, Helen Oxner, Lula Bess's grandmother Oxner," Aunt Bessie said. "The true test of a lady or gentleman, Mama Helen often swore, is to drop in on them at an awkward time—say half-past nine at night, and be unfed. See then what they do. If they're too mean to do anything but pass the visit off as a breach of manners, then you know what you have. If they give you some little snack or flummery of dessert, then you've got a little better class of folk. That has a category and name too.

But if they flash to the kitchen, set you at the table with the best in the house, and if the kitchen is clean, then that person is a gentleman or lady, and God's with the house."

"Kind of reminds me," said Kildee, "Of the Bible passage that says to be hospitable to strangers, for you might be entertaining an angel unawares."

"Exactly, Dee." Aunt Bessie rocked gently and fanned with a palmetto leaf fan. She thought awhile and said, "But it don't have to be in hopes your guest's an angel. Seems to me, it's them who ain't angels who really need the hospitality. I take no issue with the holy word, but that's the spirit of it elsewhere. Doing to the least of these, the Master said."

After a season of silence, Kildee said, "My Grandpappy Henderson always claimed that a gentleman, in the way of ownership, needed only three things to make it in the world."

Aunt Bessie asked what they were.

"First, a generous spirit and grace of heart. That would take care of hospitality. Then his grandmama's prayer book. Third, his grandpa's studbook. That's all. His life was simple that way. He didn't need a lot of things, and he'd share his last crumb."

"Yes, I knew him right well before he died, and I married Columbus Caldwell up here. He was hospitable that way. He would share his last crust with a stranger—a fine gentleman true. No matter what, he always had a ready smile and little things for us chaps. If it wasn't anything more than a peppermint drop, he'd have something for each of us every day. When one or another of us little girls had not minded like we ought to, he'd say, 'Girls, if you can't be good, at least be interesting.'"

Cousin Dana Oxner joined them on the porch. The big grandfather clock struck eight chimes from just inside the hall door.

Dana had been inside talking with Lula Bess. They'd had a lot of catching up to do. Lula Bess followed behind.

Dana had left Clay Bank County to go to college, but she and Lula Bess had kept in touch. When Dana went on to take her first job in Charlotte, she'd often come home, so the girls, now grown to be women, did the best they could to continue to share their lives and be friends. This, they'd at least moderately achieved.

The two women quietly pulled up rockers and joined Aunt Bessie and Dee, who sat silently now. The ragged line of hemlocks to the west had turned dark with the dropping sun. The tree line looked like a black paper cut-out pasted against a flat white wall.

"What y'all been talking about? Did we interrupt?" Cousin Dana asked.

"Oh no. Just how and why Aunt Bessie here is about the most hospitable lady I've ever known."

"Ain't that a fact, Dee!" said his wife.

"You know, we're blessed in Aunt Bessie here," Cousin Dana declared.

"And blessed I am too, in having family who'll come all this way to visit a lonely old widow woman who's not got long for this world." Bessie's look included all three. Dana felt that in her warm way, she seemed to embrace them with her eyes.

There was a pause. The old grandfather clock could be heard ticking just inside the door. The breeze blew down the hall and they felt the warmth from inside blown out to them. The lace curtains in screenless open windows upstairs blew outside in the breeze.

"The hills this evening sure have a pretty blue haze," Aunt Bessie commented. "Now that we've had several good rains, I can hear the creek running over its rocks again. It's a bold stream."

"Crystal clear too," Kildee observed. "I went out there this morning at dawn, took the old gourd dipper, and had me a long drink. Y'all sure have got good cold water up here. Out of the granite stone. Out of the quartz rock deep under the hills. Not like the dear old Broad River behind us at home. It gets muddy after a big rain."

"I expect half of the Upcountry washes down by your back door," Cousin Dana said. She worked in the corporate offices of a big forestry concern in Charlotte as an executive secretary. She had to deal with the few regulations that governed clear-cutting, the few rules that tried, but inevitably failed, to prevent abuse of the land.

Dana, who was a few years younger than Lula Bess, had made a good career of her secretarial skills. She was a business major at her school, did well enough, but did not rate at the top of her class. She never really liked school.

In Charlotte, she married, divorced, then stayed single

this time. She took back her maiden name. Her son was now out on his own or with his dad.

"You still liking Charlotte?" Kildee asked in a lull.

"I'm fed up with my job," she said. She'd already told Lula Bess the same. "In fact, I'm so sick of it, I could scream. The commute in and back. The nine-to-five routine, the forms to fill out in triplicate, countless papers to shuffle, most of them meaningless, the telephone or cell phone ringing, now the computer, and dozens of e-mails. I hate it all, and I hardly ever even see my boss any more. All we do is e-mail. He takes his work home, he so hates to come in. I would too if I could, believe me. It's a battle to get through the traffic in town. At least we've got marked spaces in the parking garage next to our office tower. When the boss does come in, all you see of him is his back, sitting at his blurry screen. Sometimes he still e-mails me, and me sitting next door."

There was a pause. The group was a bit jolted by the agitated tone of her voice. Then Aunt Bessie added, "Dana tells me the people ain't friendly. They're just strictly business, jostling and pushing and shoving folks, out to grab what they can. At the office, she's got few people she can talk to, much less call her friends. They don't have time for anything but getting ahead."

"That's right, Aunt Bessie, there's not much joy in that world."

There was a long pause. The lightning bugs were signaling in the laurel thickets. They lit the lawn and the giant clumps of rhododendron at its edges and high up into the trees.

"When I went to the job interview at International, the interviewer said that I'd find it easier to work than to have fun. He said I'd learn to love my job. It's a great place to work. There's no distractions at all."

To Kildee, that seemed odd, if not crazy.

"I should have read the signs right then and there," Cousin Dana said. "But my young eyes were full of the big city. I wanted what I thought was success, was ambitious to get on and wasn't listening clear."

"Your boss said it was a good place to fill out forms because there were no distractions?" Kildee repeated. "That ain't much of a world."

Cousin Dana filled Kildee and Lula Bess in on what it was like to live at Myers Park, the exclusive in-town neighbourhood of the '20s, where her salary allowed her to buy a small house. She'd moved there from Pineville, by way of Mint Hill.

"Folks measure you with the ruler of money, and with things like the cars you can buy, or where and how far and how long you take vacations. Like most people everywhere in business, they talk about cost-effectiveness and profit and loss. If you're not cost-effective to someone, you're not likely to be that someone's friend. Everyone's on the make and on the take. And people come and go like their second home was a bus or a train. Nothing stays put in Charlotte, at least not for long. It's raw and banking rich, lots of loose cash to be got, and lots of coats and ties and designer clothes. For all that, it's just an overgrown cotton mill town. Based on cash and getting ahead."

"A wannabee Atlanta, what your Cousin Charlie declares," contributed Aunt Bessie.

"Atlanta. What a place to model after!" Dana said. "We have to go there on business sometimes. I always dread going anywhere near. The place is culturally deprived, like anywhere USA. Everybody's moved out of the city, and it looks almost as sad and rundown as Ghana, where our business had to send me with the boss two years ago. The firm's gone global, you know."

Matter of fact, Kildee didn't know, and if it weren't for Cousin Dana's association with the company, he wouldn't in the least care.

The talk had continued on these lines past sunset, touching the stress of life in the city, the shallowness of relationships formed there, then shifted to more pleasant things. The purple dark found them speaking of friends and family back home whom both women knew. The clock struck ten.

In a lull, they marvelled at the stars, very bright on this clear night. The stars looked as close as the lightning bugs. Lula Bess commented that she felt a real touch of fall in the air. The warmth blowing out to them from inside the house actually now felt good. Cousin Dana got up and brought them each a cup of coffee.

Kildee was in the process of telling some humourous anecdotes about things that had happened at the store, or that he'd heard at the store. The women laughed heartily at his tales.

As was usually the case with the best storytellers back home, the teller was most frequently the butt of the joke. For who'd want to listen for long to a teller who always made himself the hero—unless it was obvious he was setting himself up in the role of a mock-hero who'd fall from grace.

Anyway, the talk got around to Triggerfoot and some of his scarey scrapes. Lula Bess told the story of Trig's finding the Revolutionary War cannon in his bottomland corn, and how it eventually got him put in jail.

Then Kildee narrated the story of Triggerfoot's hornets that got back at them who'd locked him up, exaggerating as he went, in a story that didn't need much exaggeration. The ladies got a good laugh.

Lula Bess topped off the stories with how Trig got the better of Banker McCall and ended at one and the same time both the number-one project of the do-gooders of the town—making Trig a habitat-for-humanity home—and the number-one goal of the Chamber of Commerce and State Development Board—landing a new auto assembly plant for the town.

Aunt Bessie and Cousin Dana understood the morals of these tales and agreed with Lula Bess and Kildee's assessment of the scene.

"Yes, Triggerfoot Tinsley. Now, there's a real hero. He kept y'all from probably looking just like Charlotte sprawl," Cousin Dana said.

If Chauncey or Trig himself had been there, they'd have probably added, "And living in more subdivisions of Plantation Acres that don't plant, Tanglewood with no woods to tangle, and Cedar Creek with no cedars or creek."

Then the talk quieted down. Silence again. The clock ticked from the dark hall and struck the half hour. The porch rockers rocked. Aunt Bessie hid a yawn with the back of her hand. Cousin Dana, accustomed to air-conditioning as she was, had now finally cooled off sufficiently to put down her palmetto fan.

Kildee made the first move to go to bed. After saying it three times, and still talking on, he finally did. He disappeared into the dark hall, the wood-framed screen door shutting behind, making the sound only screen doors can. It echoed down the long hall.

The ladies on the porch now alone, had some more conversation, but Aunt Bessie soon followed Kildee. Her bare arms were getting cool, and she had to do a few last little things in the kitchen preparing for breakfast, before she too could quit the scene. Her breakfasts were no skimpy, quick affairs. She always cooked a big meal even when she was there alone. With company, she had grits, ham, bacon, eggs, red-eye gravy, biscuits, and homemade fig and peach preserves. As her people always did in the summer back home, she had tea for breakfast, iced not hot. The full pitcher was already in the fridge. She put the grits on so they could soak all night and save precious breakfast preparation time.

So with Kildee in bed and Aunt Bessie bustling about in the kitchen, the two cousins now had some more time alone and shared some confidences they'd not share with anybody else. It seemed that Dana had gotten so dissatisfied with Charlotte, she'd thought she might move. She felt so alone, lost among strangers she really didn't care anything about. Among her acquaintances, she said she didn't have one friend as good as Lula Bess, whom she now seldom had the chance to see. Something was centrally wrong with that. But her good salary was the bait of the trap, a salary that could buy all those things she'd never had back home and on which she was sad to say she'd come to depend.

Before they parted for the night, Bess told Dana she ought to think about moving back to Clay Bank. They'd find her a place. Dee knew everyone.

The two went to their beds with the comfort of knowing their friendship had been once again strengthened across space and time.

The house was completely silent now. It had been a while since the two had heard the clank of pots and pans from the kitchen. Aunt Bessie had retired for a well-deserved rest. In the far distant hall, Lula Bess could faintly hear the clock's twelve chimes.

When Lula Bess entered the big upstairs bedroom where she and Kildee slept in the comfortable four-poster bed, Kildee's breathing proved him already asleep.

She undressed and slipped in quietly beside him so as not to wake him up. He looked so peaceful and at rest in that other distant world, on their far river shore. She guessed, and probably rightly, that in his dreams, he was at home.

All this, Kildee narrated to Chauncey a piece at a time at the store. Lula Bess had filled in the spaces between at a Friday-night family supper she'd invited Chauncey to. They ate in the kitchen where one of the daughters had thumbtacked the big *Welcome Home* sign that had hung at the store.

There, over a big pork roast, rice and hash, cheese pie, okra and beans, fresh biscuits, and other bounty of the land, Kildee had declared that talking to Cousin Dana about the work in the synthetic industries and corporations that looked down on his kind and his way of life, had convinced him he had nothing to be ashamed of at all. College textbooks be damned. He wasn't filthy rich, filthy, or rich, and at least he didn't slave all week just to have some few hours of leisure time. He never really separated his work from his play. Never even stopped to think it could be done. It wasn't in him to sacrifice a part of his year rushing feverishly about in order to enjoy a few weeks in a far away place. He'd find that no life at all. He didn't have to establish his manhood by wielding power over men. Walking alone by the mountain stream at Flat Rock, he'd recalled his Grandpa Henderson's saying that a man's true worth in the world depended on what kind of wake he leaves behind him as he passes through life. Grandpa one evening by the old Henderson fireplace, as he was nearing eighty years old and Kildee was just a lad, had said words that had registered with him even then. Kildee recalled the scene vividly and the old man's exact words: "A man that has the power to make other people happy is a power that makes all others appear small." Grandpa Henderson had continued: "The boasted progress of today may be valiant, but it's not especially interesting, because no kind of material greatness can ever really satisfy the heart. It can't live by bread alone."

Of late, Kildee said how it was strange that all his grandpa and father had said kept coming back to him in little sentences and phrases when he least expected them. Bess added that that's what her mother had said was a sign you were getting old, that the things way back seemed nearer than the things that happened yesterday. Cousin Dana had added how strange it was that the older she got, the wiser her parents and grandparents got.

Kildee declared to Chauncey that what Cousin Dana had said of her life in Charlotte had made tangible the problems and deficiencies of that other world, while highlighting his own blessings. It reinforced his decision to take the direction he'd been setting himself on.

No. He didn't need industrial- and corporate-bought leisure to seek what that world called culture or to, as Dana said they phrased it, "develop potential." He developed his soul in both his work and play, and culture he lived, rather than sought. It was after all not a matter of power to purchase or the accumulation of things.

On his trip, he said he'd learned even better to be thankful for what he had at home and the store. Then, when he actually returned to the country—already decided he'd keep the old place open—the big surprise homecoming had convinced him he was doing the right thing. With the good Lord's help, he figured—no, vowed—he'd keep the store open.

Hearing this straight from Kildee, Chauncey was greatly

relieved. He even sighed a detectable sigh. Bess caught the sound, and reading it rightly, smiled. Chauncey had guessed his friend had made that decision, but Kildee hadn't, until now, told him so. And he knew what Dee said that he'd do, he'd do.

The big supper and the good news made Chauncey glow. Colour suffused his forehead and cheeks. When Lula Bess offered him dessert of a homemade peach cobbler and the hand-churned ice cream one of the daughters had made, he didn't refuse. As he reached for the big heavy ironstone cobbler dish still warm from the oven's heat, he said, "Well, I've already just had one dessert, but tonight, I reckon I can make room for two!"

Bess knew what he meant, and with her eyes, agreed. She looked at her husband and said softly, "Dee, if you'll help Chauncey with the cobbler, I'll get y'all's ice cream."

XIX

Grandpa Henderson's Teachings

Next day, Chauncey stopped by the store in the afternoon to say hello and tell Kildee how much he'd enjoyed the supper and company last evening. Reflecting upon the conversation last night, he told Kildee that lately he'd been thinking a lot about things his own father had said when he was a lad.

"Funny how you remember these things," Chauncey said. "And how much they can mean to you now. They must have meant something to you then too, even though you didn't realise it, or the words wouldn't come back so clear after forty or fifty years."

"Reckon that's so," Kildee said. "When you're young you recognise somehow without the front of the brain. Maybe you're more aware than you know, and it's something like instinct that's separating what's important and lasting from what's not."

Mr. Lyman was sitting in his usual rocking chair. "God's way," he said. "You'd have to be a real fool not to see there's a plan."

"If you're listening that is," Chauncey said.

Kildee went on: "I remember Grandpa had such a gentle way of saying things. He told us children how he believed that in the long run a person couldn't lose by courtesy. He was big on manners. He always said that in the turmoil and battle of things especially, we have to keep a grace of heart. He was always talking about what he called the grace of heart that redeems human nature. I had no idea what those words meant then but can recall them just as he said them: 'The grace of heart and happy symmetry that redeem human nature.'"

Chauncey said, "I reckon he came from a time that had seen real want, and the land was in the shadow of what my grandpa called the Grand Smash of 1865."

"A real thing, that shadow," Mr. Lyman added. "It's a wonder any of us are still here. My own grandpa fought in that war and came home used up. He was never the same. It wasn't just the death of his brothers and friends or the burned-out place and starting over, but the general gloom over everything. He said it was real hard to know your own young'uns would never have things as good as you had. It was supposed to be the other way around."

"Folks today are feeling that too, they tell me," added Chauncey. "Especially in the towns."

"Maybe the three-car garage on their McMansions will have to shrink down to two, or the son's wife will have to drive the passed down BMW instead of a new," Kildee said with irony.

"This land's going to see want again," Mr. Lyman said.

Chauncey agreed, though he didn't want to inject his real predictions here. They'd have been too much of a downer, and the last thing he wanted to do today was spread gloom. Kildee's homecoming and decision to keep the store open were things to celebrate and relish. He settled for saying, "Yes, it's a lot harder to get family fortune back than to make it."

The late afternoon sun broke through the store's newly polished window panes and lit areas Chauncey'd never really seen before. There was an old homemade turkey-tail fan, the spread feathers set in a carved oak handle sitting on a pine blanket chest. A beam fell across the points of a giant deer rack mounted on the wall.

Everywhere on the farms hereabouts, people kept these stag horns and memorialised them. In Chauncey's own dining room, he had a frieze of them that seemed to fill the room with woodland memories.

It was his people's closeness to the woods and fields, Chauncey knew, that would keep them whole. Sometimes if he didn't actually hear it, the distant deep-chested music of the hounds and the far-off mellow call of the hunter's horn would come to him and sweeten his way. He felt that the real threat to the future was not so much a matter of bombs in a far off place, although he regretted them keenly, but what they were doing to their own world, the forests, water, air, and soil of home.

Chauncey listened intently as Kildee told how Grandpa Henderson had spoken of the old days of his own father, a time when there was a gentle, unstrenuous, finished sort of living, no frantic desire to get ahead, no worship of power or fame.

Kildee recalled that his grandpa would often say that the best success is being contented to enjoy life itself. Kildee concluded that his life was a product of the soil, the great river, the deep fresh woods.

"A nature-guided way," Chauncey added, understanding what Kildee meant.

"Just the other day," Kildee continued, "I was putting cans on the shelves when it popped into mind the image of Grandpa stopping from stacking firewood and taking me by the arm. I can even recall the feel of his rough calloused hands on my tender child's arm as he took me aside. 'Lyles,' he said. 'The fruits of honour are courtesy, gentleness, integrity, and charity, and honour's the only tree on which all these virtues grow. Listen to me now,' he said, and repeated it again."

Grandpa Lyles Henderson Sr. had been born in 1862, during the war in which his father was killed. Grandpa had never known him, except from what family and community were considerate enough to tell. He was born a few months after his father had died.

Kildee related how his own father, Grandpa Henderson's son, another Lyles Henderson, born in 1898 under the continuing shadow of loss and want, had told him much about Grandpa Henderson. He told him why he and his mother had chosen to name him after his grandpa and how all three would now share the bond of the same name.

Kildee had gone with his father to the hen nests that day,

and they'd gathered eggs together, the lad cradling them carefully in the crook of his arm. His father too was getting old. He looked at the gangly ten year old there in 1955 and said, "Oh son, how you'll be remembering this so many years from now."

Kildee watched the light play over his shelves, at intervals bringing this, now that box or canned good into view.

"Ah. Old times," he said after a pause. "That same day at the hen nests he told me what Grandpa Henderson had told him at my very same age. 'Grace of heart, Lyles,' he said. 'It's that you got to strive for, got to have. It's that which will make you great. You've got to learn to be great first. Then you will do great things.'"

Chauncey was transported there to the poultry yard with Kildee that half-century ago. He looked at his friend, who was gazing through his shelves and the walls of the store into a time that would never return.

Kildee broke off his reverie, looked at Chauncey and Mr. Lyman, and smiled.

"I wish I could do better at capturing how it was," he said.

To this Mr. Lyman only repeated, "Grace of heart. Kildee, you've done well."

As Mr. Lyman was the oldest one among them now, Chauncey knew Kildee needed that patriarchal blessing and said nothing himself. There was a time to talk and a time not to. It was maybe the hardest of all lessons to learn.

The three men were quiet for a space as the sun's light continued its move across the wall. There was Grandpa

Henderson's hunting horn hung on its worn and sweat-stained leather cord. Kildee noticed it there and made a mental note that he had to give it to Kildee Jr., Lyles IV. Back when Jr. was a lad, Kildee already told him much of what he'd just said to his friends, but it might bear repeating. Particularly nowadays, he knew folks needed that kind of reinforcement.

He recalled Grandpa Henderson in the last weeks of his life. He was in his nineties, blind, and bedridden, but his mind was as clear as a bell. As Kildee stood by his bedside, 'Grace of heart, Lyles,' he'd told him once again. 'Honour is the only tree on which all the virtues grow.'" At that time, it was not so much the words, as the sincerity with which they were said that had made the words stick. Maybe after all, it was that which brought the words back to mind after so many years, now at a time when he could take their full meaning in.

When Chauncey got home that afternoon and had completed his chores, he reflected back on the day. After his supper, he went to his old pine desk and placed a sheet of paper on the sloped front. He paused a moment to look at it, for he always liked the promise of the empty page. Then he dipped his pen, and the ink glistened in the lamp's light. He wrote the title "For Kildee" and followed it with words that lined themselves effortlessly.

> We string the days like beads
> To make of perfect circlet meaning tale,

That gives some sense of shapes beyond the room,
Of where the room makes shadows of itself
Across the wider landscape of the years.
In such we find the circling pattern of a life
All life,
To edge us toward the riddle ultimate
And find the story does not quantify,
Nor tell, but ask,
And asking thus,
Will show us roughly where in story line
We are,
To bring us circling back
Where we'd at first begun:
To stringing days like beads
Upon a golden circlet
Perfect and profound.

It was getting late. He could see the stars through the many-paned window in his alcove. How still the land lay in the dark. He read his verse over, made a revision here and there, and placed the sheet upon the growing pile. When he turned off the lamp, the stars grew brighter and the dark glowed luminescent and clear. He could hear the far-off sounds of beagles on a chase. Possum hunting time again. The sounds were ushering the season in. Chauncey was already nearly asleep when he turned back his covers and got in.

XX

Falling Weather

Chauncey was in his usual chair at Kildee's store. The weather had turned wet and cold, and having finished his morning chores, he'd driven in to Kildee's for a few items and, more importantly, some society. The weather had delayed his project of sinking some holes with the post hole digger to put up a new cedar post and barbed wire pasture fence. The posts, neatly sawn off his place, were trimmed and ready, but with this weather, and considering the fact that the job wasn't pressing, he'd wait for a sunny day. This decision had one thing more to recommend it. It allowed him an afternoon at the store. The fact that the store was still there and might not have been made him even more conscious of its worth.

A little after Chauncey'd arrived and made his usual salutations around, in came Trig. He'd walked briskly from his farm and was ready to "light."

Folks there were always glad to see Trig. They knew they could count on getting news you wouldn't get elsewhere, and always accompanied by a take as singular as the news itself.

After some friendly banter and talk of the weather, Kildee's sojourn in Flat Rock, the sick and shut in, crops, farm animals, politics, a few choice jokes, church news, family anecdotes, and such—the usual easy play of familiarities—Chauncey volunteered a piece of news of his own. Today, it was he, not Trig, who enlightened the scene.

Seems he'd been in to Clay Bank yesterday to get the roll of barbed wire for his fence and stopped at Ronnie B's, the local meat and three vegetables restaurant for a quick fried chicken and rice-and-cream gravy dinner before going home to his afternoon's chores. There he picked up the local county paper from the counter and began to peruse.

There never was much news in the thing, mainly photos of brides and school kids doing the usual school kids' things. The first rule of county journalism was displayed perfectly there: Get as many people's names in the paper as you can.

But today the bold front page headline ran:

EXPERT TO PLAN TOWN FUTURE!

That of course got Chauncey's attention.

Before he could tell the assembled at Kildee's any more, Trig weighed in.

"*Expert*, did you say, Chauncey? Wait. I figure I can predict the whole thing without you speaking a word. Y'all do know the meaning of *expert*, don't y'all?"

"Well, Trig, I got some idea of what the dictionary would say," was Chauncey's reply.

"*Dictionary, smicktionary,*" Trig answered. "Noah Webster's no friend of us here. I learned that quick in grade school. His talk and spelling is as foreign as France."

"Well, then, Trig, what does expert mean in your dictionary?" Spurgeon Adams asked.

"Expert," Trig said slowly and then paused, repeating the word like a child does at a spelling bee. "It just means somebody from somewhere else."

Spurgeon, Kildee, Chauncey, and the rest of the crew knew exactly what Triggerfoot meant. Seemed that Clay Bank folk in authority didn't ever trust their own for things of the "smart" kind. Chauncey felt they had a kind of Colonial mentality. If it didn't come from somewhere else, it musn't be worth anything—that is, as felt by the Chamber of Commerce, banking community, Planning Commission, Development Board kind. For these, Chauncey and Triggerfoot had no respect and often downright scorn. These all-business time-is-money sorts always had the almighty short-term dollar as the bottom line and usually had made long-term messes of all the things they'd been involved in, or at least to the minds of those at the store—those outside the pale.

"Well, boys, you know how the dictionary does it," Trig continued. "He breaks words down into their parts. And here we got two: *Ex* and *Spurt*."

Long pause.

"That's right," Chauncey agreed.

"Well, *Ex,* like an ex-wife or ex-president, is something that's over, that use to be but ain't any more. Same as useless—a has-been. And *Spurt*? Just a small leak under a lot of pressure. That's all—and won't last long—here one minute, then gone, leaving a mess somebody local that stays put has got to clean up, if ever they get the chance and they can. Sometimes it's so big a mess, and done in asphalt and concrete, that it'll be around a long, long time and require more experts to be brought in."

The men had to laugh at the truth of the thing.

"But I got a better meaning than that," Trig continued once the chuckles died down. "He's a man that knows more and more about less and less."

The men laughed again.

"And his kind of knowing ain't my kind. He's hooked up to figures, charts, graphs, and screens with his electric socket plug to work out facts that he uses to prove. He's just the opposite of me. Most of what I know and believe I and nobody else can prove—facts, figures, or screens."

"Good sense," said Kildee from over the counter as he cut off a bright orange wedge of fragrant cheese from the giant hoop. He handed it to Trig on a sheet of saltines.

"That deserves a reward," he said. "Get yourself a Co-cola and some more soda crackers. Help yourself to a can of sardines."

"Believe I will," Triggerfoot replied, getting himself an RC from the drink box. "Much obliged, Kildee, old son of the sod."

If nothing else, Triggerfoot was never shy when there was an invitation to eat. "Call me anything you want," he was often heard to say, "Long as you call me for dinner."

Trig's metabolism was sky high, about like a growing

teenage boy's. He was always doing something, kept at his chores, stayed on the move, never sat still for long. As a result, he could usually be counted on to be hungry. On his farm, he was the sole hand, or, as he would have it, one of three. "Me and the two mules," he'd say. Other times, the three were "me, myself, and I."

"So Chauncey, this-here fancy out-of-town expert, this small leak under a lot of pressure that knows more and more about less and less," Spurgeon continued. "What's he supposed to do?"

"He's to set up a ten-year plan for building a bypass round the town, court industry to a new-built industry park, develop what they call a 'tourism strategy,' and open a retirement community for what they call 'snow birds.'"

"Snow birds," repeated Mr. Lyman from where he'd been dozing in the dark of a corner. "What kind of birds is them?"

"The kind from whom experts is most likely to come," Chauncey answered. "We import them to Clay Bank to tell us how to live."

"Well, ain't that town gone plumb to hell!" Kildee observed. "The government's expensive school system's a tragedy, the sprawl of billboards looks like the whole world's on sale, and everywhere you look there are Sprawl-Marts and asphalt and deserted shopping centres closed down so more can be put somewhere else right nearby. The experts can advise to cut trees, bulldoze land, take up good farms, turn soil to concrete, build new roads and shopping centres that will shortly close down. On and on endlessly. Progress for the sake of progress, you see. It makes the money engines churn."

"And they grind up you and me," Trig volunteered.

A pause.

"Making another full-fledged Kingdom of Thingdom like thousands across the land," Chauncey added.

Then another long pause.

"Them old deserted shopping centres look like ghost stores," Mr. Lyman declared. "Plate-glass windows broke out, plywood boarding them up, and just a mile away, the bulldozers working to build another new one; one that'll look just the same as the old one, only bigger, but will still have the same Chinese goods."

"Wonder why they pick on the best, richest soil that's growing good peanuts or corn to seal over with asphalt?" Chauncey asked in true puzzlement. "This new Sprawl-Mart took over the finest peach orchard that made the sweetest peaches I counted on, looked forward to, every summer that went by. I marked time of the year by those peaches." Chauncey had a look of loss in his eyes.

"No more of that now," Kildee said. "Soon you'll be getting little hard knots of peaches from California with no taste at all in the grocery part of the Sprawl-Mart Super Store right where them good peaches used to be raised."

"Reckon I won't," Chauncey declared. "I'll do without first."

"Me either," Trig agreed. "I don't have cash money period. If I don't grow it, or can't trade for it, I don't eat it. I've got half a dozen peach trees, always full. Peaches fall on the ground for the deer to eat. You can have some of them. I never am able to use 'em all even after I've canned them up and made peach brandy too."

"Reckon I'll put me in a couple of trees too," said Chauncey after a pause. "You know how much I like to plant trees."

"Good idea, and till yours make, I'll supply you, Chaunts old friend," and Trig wasn't just talking to hear himself talk. He made no idle promises. He'd remember his vow come next July. As he said of his abundance of beans, it gave him pleasure to be able to give things to his friends.

The evening passed on with such conversation. The talk moved slow and easy, a weave of stories within stories reminding of more—tales that dodged and detoured and went around hills but never found a dead end, conversation that perambulated, peregrinated, and sashayed, unregimented, following no templates, no orchestrated plot, no ruler-drawn efficient line. As the sky darkened and the weather turned even more raw, an occasional pelting of sleet hit the old building's roof tin.

"Would you listen to that!" Mr. Lyman declared. "My granddaughter better come get me, 'fore the roads get too bad."

"Don't worry, Mr. Lyman," Kildee assured. "If she can't, she knows we'll get you home."

Chauncey decided he'd best carry Trig on back, then get on home himself to the chores. They prepared to leave.

The day dwindled down into grey. The store's naked solitary light bulb hanging from the ceiling got brighter as the sky turned more leaden and a volley of sleet hit the tin.

"Falling weather," Kildee had rightly predicted this

morning as he first set out and then again some hours ago.

"Going to snow sure," he'd said. "See how the smoke from Miss Mattie Lou's chimney is laying heavy and close to the ground."

"Yep," Trig said to Chauncey as they left the store. "Kildee foretold this weather just right. Didn't need satellite printouts, nor degrees, nor instruments, nor weather charts, nor graphs, nor Doppler Radar. And nobody excepting one who lives here like him could read those same signs. Now there's a real expert if you ask me."

"A local one too and an expert because he is," agreed Chauncey, as the old door shut behind. And the threshold that merged two worlds, already worn smooth with the passing of many generations of feet, was crossed one more time.

As they walked to his truck, Chauncey turned to look over his shoulder at the store, as if needing assurance it was still there. Through the window, he could see Kildee's figure moving in silhouette beneath the naked bulb.

The dark of the sky, by contrast, made the light brighter inside. He could hear laughter. Muffled as it was, he picked out Mr. Lyman's own.

"Better get you on home," he told Trig. "It's starting to snow." The flakes had begun to fall gently. They stuck to the hood of the truck, and Trig, noticing, rightly predicted there'd be snow on the ground next day.

XXI

Round the House and Mind the Dresser

The dancing would begin before too long now. The old Henderson place high on the hill bluff overlooking the silent river had several big hearth fires burning this grey winter evening, so the double doors to the long front porch could be thrown open. Doing so would add another fifty feet for dancing the reels, thus circling out from the spacious parlour through the big central hall, and then on outside.

It was just one week to the day after the biggest snow the county had experienced in quite awhile had brought life to a standstill in Clay Bank town, the snow Kildee had predicted would come that day at the store. Out here, things had moved along about as always though. Most everybody had trucks, and the snow on the roads hadn't lasted long. Two warm days of sun, and only a few traces of it remained in the shade.

Kildee was just propping open the heavy pine doors of the house with Grandmama Verna McMorries Henderson's smoothing irons. They did proper new duty now, practically, functionally, and as links of remembrance, like so many of the old ways in the Henderson household. There, nothing genuine was ever thrown away that could be put to use. Coming as they did with the ghosts of hands who'd touched them, the irons served more than utilitarian duty.

The dancers would soon be shifting, turning, all in a continuous, weaving line. Kildee could see them in his mind's eye. He was in his shirt sleeves, his flannels rolled up on his forearms to reveal the white weave of thermals beneath. Having worked up some heat in the preparations, he showed a few drops of sweat on his brow.

Chauncey greeted him from the porch steps. He'd had a quiet walk up the hill from the store. Kildee closed midafternoon to get ready for tonight. Chauncey had parked below the store, so in his walk, he could traverse the entire cross roads. The one-room post office sat behind him next to the defunct cotton gin. He walked past the two one-room cement block buildings for hunters to spend the night, over one of which Kildee, in humourous mood, had nailed a hand-lettered sign. *Henderson Hilton* it read. Then his way led past an old boarded-up store and an empty big two-storied building made of logs and covered with clapboards black with time. It was so old, nobody knew exactly when it was put there. But rumour was that it was in its origins also a store and trading post in the days of the first settlers and Indian trading. It had weathered two wars fought around it. It had seen Redcoats and Patriots, Bluecoats and Confederates alike. Chauncey always thought of the building as the ghostly patriarch ancestor of the present Kildee's store. It was venerable and enduring, having witnessed and survived the Grand Smash of 1865, a time when his grandfather said of the younger generation after the war that pretty much the whole of life was merely not dying. Now, the building's empty cavernous interior echoed hollowly the sounds of its newer counterpart that itself still wasn't new. As Chauncey walked by, he could hear in the wind the creek of shutters and doors opening and slamming on its second floor.

But the foremost reason he'd parked back at the store was so he could watch the river materialise out of the interwoven tops of its river trees as he climbed uphill slowly, measuring his steps against the view, hearing his feet crunch on the gravel path. A fine scene it was, quiet for contemplation, for savouring. Chauncey felt how it would be so different an hour hence when the players were all tuned and the people's feet itching to dance.

"I hear Joe-Pratt tuning his fiddle, so I must be about on time," Chauncey declared to Kildee as he came up to the porch.

"Just in time," Kildee replied. "To help me move a few pieces of furniture out of the way."

"Glad to."

The custom was to pick up the parlour furniture from the middle of the room and line it against the walls. All impediments to the most rambunctious moves were thus cleared out of the way.

The fiddle measured out snatches and scraps of song. He

caught the sweet and melancholy tune "Women of Ireland," then a few bars of their own Singin' Billy Walker's "Promised Land." It was a slow warm up for the fervour to come.

Lula Bess was bringing in the two punch bowls for the hot spiced mull that had been heating on the kitchen stove. Two were needed, one for the mull "with," and the other for the mull "without." The "without" one, which they called Presbyterian punch, was much smaller, mainly only a gesture, for there were few who'd come this mid-December night who'd feel the need to go without.

Christmas was a-coming, as the old song declared, but tonight, in some ancient, atavistic way, this was as big a time of the year, the dividing mark between old and new year. It was the solstice, shortest day of the year, and at 5:30, it was already about dark.

Chauncey could hear Joe-Pratt's friend Brian Kelly tuning his mountain dulcimer, then accompanying Joe-Pratt with a few tentative snatches of song.

Chauncey had brought a gallon of his best scuppernong wine. He had the glass jug crooked by a finger of his right hand as he gave it over to Lula Bess, who would add it to the table of drinks and slices of cold ham and baked turkey, domesticated and wild. These were now being laid out on large ironstone platters on a table in a corner of the great hall. Next to them was a small plate of roasted quail that one of the Blair boys had shot on a hunt the day before. They were smoke roasted, each with a neat piece of bacon curled around.

Bess had placed her great-grandma Helen Eison's tall

candelabras at either end of the table to lead the revellers on. A pine bloom coverlet was spread as tablecloth. It was a dark indigo blue, woven by her Grandma Blair. A white linen cloth elaborately embroidered with gold silk thread was centred in the middle. An old silver bowl in which floated red, pink, and white camellias added the finishing touch.

"Not Christmas without camellias," Lula Bess said. She'd just cut the white ones from the *Alba Plena* that Kildee's great grandmother had planted in the yard. The snow hadn't burned its glowing petals at all. The Chinese red *Wahrattas* and *Professor Sargents* against their glossy green leaves were perfect for the season. She had rooted these herself from her grandmother's trees the year she and Kildee married.

Chauncey and Kildee moved the mahogany sofa under the parlour's pair of front windows.

Chauncey felt the sharp eagle's claw carving on the feet where his hand gripped.

"They made 'em solid in those days," Kildee declared.

"And heavy too," Chauncey agreed as he mopped at his brow with his bandana.

Joe-Pratt and Brian sat on low wooden stools, their backs to the fire, making the final adjustments to their strings. The sofa now in its new place, Kildee declared their work done.

"Sounds like somebody's foot on the porch," Kildee declared as they'd finished their chore. "I'd know that stride anywhere." And he was right. Chauncey recognised it too.

In came their friend Triggerfoot carrying a small jug in one hand and his banjo in the other.

"How's all y'all doing this blackest, brightest night of the year?" he asked as he looked expansively around, taking them all in. "I do hope you're ready for the bedazzlement to come."

"I believe we're up to it," answered Chauncey.

"Long as the punch holds out," Trig declared. "My banjo will too." When Kildee had invited him last week, he'd simply said *B.B.* All he needed to, for Trig knew it stood for *Bring Banjo*, and that he had. Folks declared they were glad to see he had it with him.

"Hope that voice of yours hasn't been sterilised by your latest batch," Chauncey said.

"Sterilising ain't even in my vocabulary, Chaunts old man, least not for this one more year."

Trig drew up the cane-bottomed straight chair he'd made as a gift one Christmas for Lula Bess and Kildee. It had an honoured place at the Henderson hearth. He sat down with banjo on his knee and immediately set in to tune. He took his time, getting it right. The new temperature and atmosphere made it tricky hard.

"How y'all boys tonight?" he asked Joe-Pratt and Brian. They assured him they were ready for any musical mayhem he might be likely to commit.

As they bantered, the men recognised Clint Blair's voice from the kitchen, talking to Lula Bess. He'd delivered some deviled eggs and sliced cold baked meats from his sisters and sister-in-law. He told Lula Bess they'd be on directly with their husbands and young'uns, in full complement.

The men in the parlour greeted Clint as he entered the

room. His cheeks were red from work outdoors in the cold. His blue eyes sparkled with merriment and mischief.

Tonight he'd brought Ida with him. She was in the kitchen helping Lula Bess. They could hear her cheery voice. She made a big banana pudding, Clint's favourite, and had just turned it over to Bess. Ida Jessine Alston, the new joy of his life.

She was farmer Aiken O'Kelley Alston's youngest and went to his church. They'd always been quietly friendly since childhood days. Off at college, he thought he'd almost let her get away, but, truth to tell, she never got too serious with anyone, guessing in her intuitive way that it would one day dawn on the thick-headed boy that he had feelings for her. She sure had 'em for him.

So now having received what he liked to call his homecoming degree, and putting his life successfully in order as the vet around there, they'd gotten serious, real serious, and tonight they'd decided to announce their engagement and marriage plans. The dance would provide a fitting place and a perfect time. The old year and old sorrows and the dark stood diminishing before the New Year, happiness and light, a new start, and a new life to come.

Clint made a beeline to Chauncey and asked him to step outside with him. He had a serious favour to ask.

Chauncey obliged. He could always tell when there was something on Clint's mind and followed him straight.

"Chaunts, I've been trying all week to see you. I came over this morning, but you must have been out planting trees. I wanted to ask if you'll stand for me at the wedding?"

"Well, how will Joe-Pratt feel?"

"I've already talked to my brothers about it, and they all say you're the right one."

At that, Chauncey paused. "Then you know I will," he said.

"Wouldn't want anybody else."

The two stood silent for a while. Clint was about to say something when Lula Bess came out in a hurry and asked him to help move a table. "Need your strong back," she said. The two followed her in.

The next half-hour saw the arrival of Carolan Glenn with his guitar, Billy Sims with a mandolin, and a second fiddler, talented young Dan Connelly O'Dooney, who'd driven forty miles to be there. He was a friend of Joe-Pratt's, who was himself known in fiddle circles as a real master with a reputation beyond their community's fields. That's how Connelly knew Joe-Pratt and used every chance he could to make music with him.

In that same half-hour, about a dozen friends had joined the gathering. There were another dozen on the road, and still another dozen more leaving their doors at home. The procession was stately enough in its way. It was topped off with Mark Milling who brought his bow dulcimer, and O'Rion Russell with the small pipes he was learning to play.

The musicians set into spirited versions of "Shady Grove" and "Old Rosin the Beau," then an even more spirited "Whiskey in the Jar" and the "Cotton-Eyed Joe" that some of the oldest there still called "McLeod's Reel." "Billy in the

Low Grounds," "Fisher's Hornpipe," and "Jenny Get Your Hoe-Cake Done" were the signal to start pairing and get ready for a reel.

Before they set in, however, it was left to Kildee to welcome the group, and give out the rules of the night. His greeting was simple and heartfelt: "Welcome friends!" Some of the guests answered him back. His rules were just as simple. "Round the house and mind the dresser," he declared, and all knew the traditional meaning withal. They could dance all over the house, but he was half-heartedly cautioning the overeager ones among them to be mindful of smashing up the furniture and to look out for Bess's breakables. He said this with a wink of the eye, however, as if encouraging them to come right up to that point though, and if they exceeded it a little, not to worry a whole lot. All would be forgiven, his wink said; you're among friends. *Live and let live* was in everything Kildee did.

It was full dark now and those coming up the path could hear the music from far down the hill. As they got closer, they could see the welcoming glow of lights and hear on the wind the bright sound of women's laughter, the occasional spirited "Kip!" and "Hup!" of a dancer or musician.

The players, now gathered nine strong, went through all the exuberant reels, jigs, and waltzes they knew. They also played some old favourite tunes for the dancers to weave intricately patterned square dance quadrilles, with Kildee standing on a sturdy old chair doing the calls. There were even solos from Trig, singing two of his Billy Walker tunes in his rich baritone, to the acclaim of all. On these, he was joined by Joe-Pratt and Connelly on their fiddles in finest form.

About eleven o'clock, Kildee hushed the crowd, and Clint, with his arm about Ida's waist, made their announcement, to embraces and congratulations and the delight of the ladies around.

"One more slow-witted man has come to his senses and finally seen what to everyone else was as plain as the nose on a face," Lula Bess declared and looked over at Ida.

"He had a little help in that, I expect," Chauncey added, and Ida blushed and smiled in her innocent way, knowing full well Clint indeed had had some coaxing from both Lula Bess and Chauncey too.

A while after the announcement and the great glee it occasioned, Chauncey with his brow flushed from dancing and the heat of the fire and the warmth of punch and Trig's jug, went outside.

He walked down the steps of the back porch and stood silently in the dark, looking at the stars. It was a clear winter's night with only the tiniest sliver of moon. He could see the full corona of the old moon in the new one's arms. The absence of moon made the stars even brighter and the blackness of the sky to glow.

He stepped outside the rectangles cast on the ground by the windows' light and relieved himself. The flux of his body smoked in the cold. *Another little country pleasure*, he said to himself, *not having to aim at a hole*. Then he was deep in thought, like he'd really want to be oblivious of all, to walk off into the black and never return. To be without thought. He thought of Hoyalene and touched her locket at his chest. The old ache was still there. He guessed it always would. Not too bad to walk off into the great dark where Hoyalene and all his closest family were. His father had died in 1974, his mama two years before his pa. His only brother had died the year before he was born and was never even known. Hoyalene had died twenty-three years ago, and it still seemed like yesterday.

The sounds of "Did You Ever Go a-Courtin', Uncle Joe, Uncle Joe" entered into his consciousness, and he could hear the laughter of the ladies and the rich tones of Trig, Kildee, Billy Sims, O'Rion Russell, and Clint joined in song. He could also hear Hoyalene's sister Clarsie and Lula Bess too. ". . . Uncle Joe, Uncle Joe . . ." The new sweet tones of Ida Alston entwined themselves with all. Ida Alston, soon to enter the family communion as Ida Blair.

"It *is* a good world," he whispered. Remembering all the pain his Hoyalene had had to endure when her great zest for life had even vanquished the high doses of morphine and she surfaced again and again from her sleep to cry out in pain for the Lord to have mercy on her. That over and over for days till the end, echoing the ancient *Kyrie. Kyrie eleison, Christe eleison, Kyrie eleison . . .*

She was better off, he knew, in a better place in a perfect realm where no sorrows were, no pain, a place that could never be known or even imagined below. But he just hated what she had to go through, and for so long. Waking to scream out in pain. At the last, she'd had that fixed stare, looking with eyes that couldn't close. When they said she was gone and they had left him alone with her, he tried to close her eyes, but they wouldn't.

So he left them that way, as he must. The recollection still seared after the score of years and caused him to utter a little muffled cry of pain. A tear wet his cheek.

Now the strains of "Cotton-Eyed Joe," and he could see the shadows of the dancers cast on the lawn in the rectangles of light from the windows. They moved in dark pantomime, the dark and light reversed. He could hear Trig's banjo plain and distinct. He flat-picked like his grandpappy. Some of the older ones in the crowd had known Grandpa Tinsley and made the connection. It was his grandpa's homemade instrument that he used, and he played the same old tunes and in the very same way. Chauncey tried to focus on that.

The dancers, despite their zeal in the frolic, were doing as Kildee had asked and were minding the dresser. Nothing was falling to smash on the floor. Tears were on Chauncey's cheeks in earnest now, and he turned his back to the scene. He had to get hold of himself.

"It *is* a good world," he said once again, and thought, qualifying the statement, "If you have no great pain, a pain that blocks out everything, possibilities and all, and with no hope of earthly life beyond it." Now he stared out into the dark with eyes like Hoyalene's own.

What a comfort the dark is, he thought as he looked beyond the stars into the void. He paused a long while. *Here, we'll never know.* Hoyalene had that knowledge now, but she couldn't vouchsafe it to him from beyond the sharp edge. He had the usual man of faith's belief that he'd see her again. But at moments like this, he wondered. And if so, in what shape, in what form? Still her bright smile shone.

I know that my Redeemer liveth, the stately lines declared. *And in my flesh shall I see God.* "Yes," he said aloud and turned toward the light inside.

He was finally coming to understand his grief was more about himself than Hoyalene. She was well somewhere, and it was he who suffered pain.

The light from the windows shone on his wet cheeks, and he saw Ida and Clint on the porch out of the windows' beams. They'd come out away from the crowd to steal a few private moments to themselves. He saw them kiss and thought of the promise he'd made Hoyalene as she died, one of the last requests she'd had the strength to make of him. "Take care of Clint. See him through," she'd asked him, knowing that their pa had died and little Clint was taking it hard and Chauncey had lost his own mother and father too. Chauncey had promised. How could he not? And it had been a pleasure and one of the ways he'd been drawn from the deep well of grief. Perhaps she knew this would happen too. He didn't know what he'd have done without Clint.

He felt good about his promise and the way he'd stood by Clint, the son he and Hoyalene had wanted so bad but couldn't have. He remembered his father's old saying, "Ain't the dog in the fight, but the fight in the dog." Clint had that fight, and Chauncey was satisfied he'd turned out well. He was a spirited, common sense lad, just like he'd have wanted a son of theirs to be.

Yes, this fostering had been as good for Chauncey as it had for Clint. And now, tonight, Clint had asked him to be his best man, and the day he and Ida had chosen was Hoyalene's own birthday.

The reel of life, with a weave of intricate knots and long flowing patterns, like the great twisting and turning, deep flowing river below, like the mystic interlaced designs on the gold decorated Gospels of Kell and Lindisfarne that he loved so well—no beginning, no end. Now men and women throughout the house were dancing to fiddle music in these same woven patterns, or mirroring the leaping and dipping ripples on the river, its waters lit by winter starlight and infant moon. In Chauncey's mind, the dancers frolicked like waves, the sea coming and going with the tide's ebb and flow, rippling up even so far as to reach the river's banks outside, connecting them with the main that had brought their people here from the old land, the green shamrock world, to the new green valley of their home.

Wasn't this the same circled pattern of comings and goings, and of darkness and light, the bright of the windows with the ebony spaces between, or the reversed shadows of the living in moving pantomime on the lawn? It was this vision of things flowing, life in flux, with its juxtapositions of opposites, with its weavings and crossings and recrossings without beginning or end that now dominated Chauncey's mind and blocked out all else. The knowledge came like a blinding light.

As he walked toward the steps, he could only image the living scene now superimposed over the mystic hatchings and crosshatchings on the glowing pages of Kell. Conjoinments. Connections and crossings to a pine bloom coverlet design. The dark and the light, the old land and new, the young and the old, dyings and marryings and births, the living, the dead, and the reborn, the known world and the unknown, stately reel processionals to the flat-picked banjo.

"Well, *there* you are!" Ida said. "We'd wondered where you'd got to."

"Sure hoped you'd not taken it into your head to leave early and go home," Clint added. "The night's still young. Still a lot of fun to be had."

"Leave now?" Chauncey replied. "Not hardly!" He spoke in tones genuinely hearty and bluff, full of accord.

As he made the porch, Ida linked his left arm and Clint his right, then ushered him across. As they reached the open door, Chauncey was aware it was now deep into Advent. As they stood there quietly a moment, listening to the sounds of the merry crowd inside, he knew he must keep awake in the long watch, for the true light was coming near.

In the doorway, they watched the intricate mazes of reel spilled out and spread before them in the hall, the full bright banquet table behind, where at each end the two clusters of candles burned. The embroidered linen cloth in the centre of the table reminded him of an altar, especially the one at which he and Hoyalene had knelt. In the candlelight, its designs moved in a dizzying way.

Panis Angelicus, the words of Aquinas came to him out of his Latin studies. The twinings of golden embroidery on the table seemed to Chauncey to be in rhythm with the wheeling constellations, only closer, brighter, and warmer than their cold gleam. They mirrored the mazes of dance. He closed his eyes for a moment. *O res mirabilis* flowed in his mind like the great starlit river outside.

Chauncey was a little unsteady on his feet. It was as if he were newly on water in a rocking boat and hadn't gotten his sea legs yet. His head swam and buzzed a little. Maybe he'd had a bit too much of Trig's jug. His steps now were tentative, and he decided to stand still and steady himself.

Clint and Ida didn't rush him. So upon the threshold itself, he paused again one last time and looked back over his shoulder at the stars above the far dark hill across the river, beyond which he imagined the crooked stone crosses within the massive granite wall of the Blair cemetery standing silver in starlight, with still a trace of snow in their shadows, and thought then again *Let us cast off the works of darkness and put on the armour of light.*

Ida smiled up at him and brushed the moisture from his cheek. Clint's arm went to his friend's shoulder as they approached the door. From inside, the brightness, the warmth and joyous sounds of the company hit him full force. It was like a driving warm rain to thawing fields. Then the three, arms interlaced, crossed the threshold, worn paper thin by those many gone before. Chauncey leaned forward into his going, like a runner greeting the tape at the end of a marathon.

L'Envoi
Gleanings

~◦~

Chauncey's Rendering from the Seventh Century Gaelic

Grant me grace to find—
Son of the living God—
Sod that's fertile, seasoned home
To make it my abode.

Crystal river silent, deep
To flow beside the place,
To wash my sins, refresh my soul
By sanctifying grace.

Deepest woodlands circling,
Shielding winter wind,
Twining branches for the birds
Before it and behind.

And all I ask of housekeeping—

I get and pay no fees;
Peas from garden, poultry, game,
Perch and bream and bees.

My share of clothing and of food,
From Lord of fairest face,
Gift to sit at times alone
And pray in every place.

Chauncey to His Books

My fathers are content to wait my time
To sit with them and call their names,
To trace their words when walking in the world.
I come to them; they cannot come to me.
My mothers likewise keep the hearth
Where hearts can gather in security
And silence reign to speak without the words.

The fathers and the mothers of my choice.
We choose our parents certainly,
Choice here, discrimination there.
They do not shout to hail us,
Speak only through ourselves,
And anchor us in place
Around which universes spin.

The Ploughman's Reverie

The mind relaxes
As it enters rhythm,
Steps on soil.
The cleaving furrough
Makes rough walking
But for groove when reverie comes
And all a life's rehearsed
Before it and within.
And then to glide
Of thoughts of week end's afternoon
When in old truck
We're all go bobbing in to town.
These thoughts ploughed in
To richen soil
Augmenting sweat that drops from brows.
The furrough is a perfect place for reverie,
No better place to plant life's dream
Or understanding of its worth
In cleaving of the earth.
The ploughman plants his reverie
And tills it under new-turned earth
To flower as the hope of home.

Old Farmer Lyman's Maxims for Modern Times

Better red neck
Than nervous wreck.
Better clodhopper
Than blade dodger.
Better song of lark
Than shot in the dark.
Better country furrough
Than city rut.
Better breath, sweat, and blood
Than monoxide and crud.
Better life that's not neuter
Than on-line computer.
Better greetings that matter
Than office's chatter.
Better honeybee drones
Than office's clones.
Better pancakes and syrup
Than poison of gossip.
Better hand in soil
Than freighter of oil.
Better dirt under nails
Than business that fails.
Better cedar and pine
Than assembly line.
Better speaking direct

Than psyche that's wrecked.
Better nap in shade
Than Super Bowl played.
Better creaking porch swing
Than Las Vegas fling.
Better cuffs that are frayed
Than to sleep half afraid.
Better biscuits at dawn
Than cellular phone.
Better bottle in front of me
Than frontal lobotomy.
Better sowing of seed
Than garden of greed.
Better sweet cream and butter
Than to live in the gutter.
Better work with your son
Than meet on the run.
Better one field well turned
Than craftsmanship spurned.
Better own well-known tillage
Than vague global village.
Better beagles' legation
Than Big Brother's new nation.
Better feet on soil
Than traffic-jam broil.
Better flood and drought
Than job in doubt.

Better fear of God
Than overlord's rod.
Better user than tool;
Better farmer than fool.

Chauncey to His Stray

A country dog that's thrown away
Adopts a place because it has no dog.
The place needs it,
Like it needs place.
A farmhouse needs a dog
And dog knows that
As well as we.
So in comes staggering nameless—
A rack of bones that's deep in years
Without a yard and set of steps to guard.
The master of the place
(His master, should he choose)
Another mouth to feed
But knows he will at last
Go forth with crust of bread,
And finally share his steak.

Chauncey's Poem on His Fortieth Birthday

Two-thirds through man's three score ten
Rows are shorter
Start to blend
With far horizon,
Distant trees.

The jug of tea
Is in the shade.
The fiddle waits
For songs long played.
The mule is tired.
So are we.
Ham-biscuits wait
Beneath the tree.

Short rows give time
To relish prime
To sit beside the fire
And doze.

To tell the tales
Without the ends
To narrate circling to the friends
And with no rush to close.

Chauncey's Song

The seasons' rhythm is a song.
Leaves fall
To prompt the buds to bloom.
By such, we count the meter of our days.
The day and night,
The rise of sun and set
Are but a rhyme.
The generations link into an epic's tune.
We plough a set of rows
Which are a couplet neat
And turn to plough two more.
The lines of verse or soil
But turn and turn to make a dance.
The fertile pairing of a man and wife
But parses out the song of life.
Habits, features, faces, gestures of our kin
Alliterate to pageant promenade.
And life in age whose folding
Back to bud to bloom again
Is universal metric pulse.
The finger on the vein
Can tell all time,
The metronome to keep us on our way.
You walk an early path,
Retrace your steps at end of day,
And make a dance across the years.

The years themselves
Repeat themselves.
And all our duty is to sing,
With song expression and the sign
Of oneness with the world.
We chant our incantation,
Sing with ease,
The joining of the scattered shards.

Rain in March

Robins call to punctuate
Sibilant whispers of rain.
Lenten lilies droop with wet,
A raucous crow flies over scene.
The blue of roman hyacinth
Reminds of blue of sky
Forgotten since in days of rain.
The world has turned to shallow sea,
With greening grass between the waves.
The Quaker Ladies seem to float
Like Noahs in their floods.
Dripping cedars hang their branches low
And mud collects on violets.
Your tennis shoes will stand no chance;
Wet socks are up to dry,
And you stay in
To watch the world
Through glass
With slower eye.

Swallowtail Summer

August comes on wings.
Vincas and phlox,
Lantanas too and zinnias
And the four o'clocks,
They all can tempt.
The iridescent blue
Of Spice's eyes
Reminds of peacocks on the lawn,
The Tiger black and yellow
Looks like modern art.
Zebra needs the pawpaw,
Thus is rare,
But when it does appear
We mark it on a calendar
Or somewhere in the brain.
And wondered where the pawpaws were.

Needs

Each time I see a Zebra Swallowtail,
I wonder where the pawpaws are.
The Zebra needs the pawpaw,
Which is rare,
And we need pawpaws by the ton.
Let's level town
To make a pawpaw farm.

Gardenias in Bloom

Blossoms touched by noonday sun
Send heavy fragrance round.
New startling white,
With yellow and ecru,
And all on self-same bough.
Blossoms glowed
Like perfect ghosts
Last evening into night
In final quartered moon.
With scented hours, flowers passing into gold,
Tomorrow tattered,
Next day brown and dry, petals paper thin
Like shrinking flesh
On which the veins stand forth
A mystic acronym,
Acrostic with no key,
Fourth day to fall.

One branch holds history
At a glance,
The spent with new.
Fast to flower
Fast to fade,
With darkest leaves
Bright shining in the sun
Through winter, summer same.

Things that pass
And things abide:
Quick flowers fleshlike, fleeting, frail
With which our finitude can halfway deal—
We as the dust from off a moth's grey wing.
But leaves that last in shining green
And do not fail
Are spirit riddles past the night,
And past the spring,
Beyond all finite minds of men.

Quietus

When songs don't come
The mind can rest.
Songs take away the peace
And make you pace.
Sometimes our brains must lull
Into a single monotone,
The hum of going deaf,
White noise,
The snow of TV sign-off in the night.
Sometimes the mind must vegetate,
Grow sloppy fat,
Eat M&M's
And brownies by the pound,
Drink extra cream in coffee,
Double-thick milkshakes.
The diet of a rhyme,
A clean-turned line
Are like the extra workout set
Or added mile.
I do not want them now,
When sprawling at his ease
Affixed to lounge chair in the den
The little music man inside
(Except for snore)
Is silent for the time,
His cheeks puffed out
With custards, cakes, and pies.

Persimmon Fall

A time for flickas' feast,
Grey-speckled backs
Race up and down
On bark that mirrors theirs.

They shake their choosy heads,
Inspect,
Rejecting this and that,
And sharpen beaks.

Fat orange fruits
Hang all around
With purpling leaves
Against a summer sea of sky.

Chauncey's Ballad of the Hawthorn Tree
      (to the Tune of the Wexford Carol, Irish Traditional)

I walked so slowly out of door.
It was a lonesome walk alone.
The one I'd loved was gone away,
She will return now never more.
     She took my very heart away
     And left an emptiness full sore.
     The hawthorn tree, it bloomed again,
     Its red the red of deep heart's blood.

I watched the sun play with the clouds,
The light in focus on the blooms:
Bare branches yet before the leaf
Revealed the bitter thorns of noon.
     As I walked out, I sang the song
     Of briers, thorns, and nettle's sting.
     I saw not clover's greening bright
     Or nesting bird with moss, on wing.

The hawthorn tree would flaunt its bloom
Red joy of love, red ache when gone,
Where pairing birds as safe from hawk
Played in and round among its thorns.
     As I walked out spring's early day
     I thought of petals stripped from bough.

As drift to earth, they fall and fall
No fruit to fashion on the bough.

Past spring I walk a slower pace
The days are shortening down to one.
I walk with none beside me now
Nor will until my breath is done.
    For then, there waits a hawthorn tree
    With reddest flowers on the stream.
    I'll cross it with a surer tread
    And gather petals for a bed.

Solstice

The year is dead;
The sun skulks
At horizon's line.
It cannot lift its head
To meet you as you walk
With ax on back
And boots made heavy
From the day.

I do not know
The winter's depths,
But glimpses have
In monotone grey sky,
Bare limbs in black,
The wind among the seed pods
Of the weeds,
Dry and rattling,
Stoic in the cold.

Like shooting stars
Cold raindrops shine
Against an ink-dark sky.

The robins lift in unison.
They circle in bright cedar grove

With gentling and unhurried cry.
They move on swiftly
But without alarm.

Full Christmas Moon

People are cajoled to open doors,
Enchanted from their walls
To stride blue-shadowed walks.
Eyes can't look away
From heavy circle of a year.

Landscape leans and yearns.
Farm's own free-range brood
Line topmost limb of cedar tree.
They look like row of ditto marks precise.
Their heads all face in mirrored same
The magnet moon.

With pea brains small, in light of day,
They cannot find their way through fence
Or think to fly above.
But here they sit
With proper reverence,
Like congregation rapt, intent,
Or chastened children in a row at school,
Expectant half, like all who see
This heavy circle of a year.
What must their pea brains think?
Perhaps they don't
And only bask in light of orb,

Attracted in the sway
Like tides.

Like unborn in the swelling belly yet,
We all yearn to the Christmas moon.
Light of life
Come down to earth
To save from dark and death.

Cranesbill

Eyes with winter weary,
Downcast with cold,
See pink among the dun.
It's cranesbill's pink
And flower's first,
Raised high on spindly stem alone,
Like kerchiefed head on craning neck
To turn in breeze,
Look this, then that,
Seeking after sun.

The cranesbill wakes
And brings surprise of spring
Full-blown.
"She's here, she's here,"
The winter weary chime—
Full-blown and pink
With head raised high,
And searching after sun.

Chauncey's Inscription for His Wood

Here poet Chauncey girdled pines
To make a hardwood forest without lines.
The lines he made with father's plough
And with his pen in rhymes set down.

May wood full grown vouchsafe you peace
Its oaks and ashes, poplars, beech,
The blessing of strong life and calm,
On banks of fern to find fit balm.

If any, Chauncey seek in after times,
Must search within his woods and lines.

Doolittle

Morgan Doolittle = Thirza Kelly "Toddie"
(1828-1918) | (1830-1909)

William Walker Doolittle = Eileen Rogers
(1870-1944) | (1877-1949)

Dixon "Dickie" = Garraphelia "Garrie"
Jeter Hardy | Sims Douglas

Chauncey Rogers Doolittle = Frances Carolina Hardy
(1910-1974) | (1911-1972)

Jeter Sims Doolittle
(1944-1948)

Chauncey Doolittle = Hoyalene Blair
(1949-) | (1959-1984)

m. 1978

Oxner

Renwick Oxner = Helen Oxner

Katharine "Kat" Oxner = Eison Blair
(1910-1987) | (1907-1981)

Bessie Oxner = John "Columbus" Cal⋯
(1918-) | (1911-1983)

Burrell Oxner = Jane Sims
(1908-1983) |

Dana Oxner
(1949-)

Lula Bess Blair Henderson = Kildee Henderson
(1949-) | (1945-)

Blair

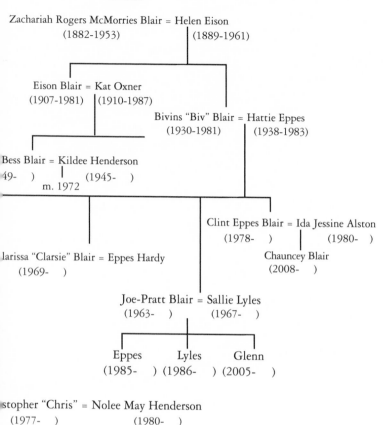

Zachariah Rogers McMorries Blair = Helen Eison
(1882-1953)   (1889-1961)

Eison Blair = Kat Oxner
(1907-1981)   (1910-1987)

Bivins "Biv" Blair = Hattie Eppes
(1930-1981)   (1938-1983)

Bess Blair = Kildee Henderson
49-   ) | (1945-   )
        m. 1972

Clint Eppes Blair = Ida Jessine Alston
(1978-   ) | (1980-   )
        Chauncey Blair
        (2008-   )

larissa "Clarsie" Blair = Eppes Hardy
(1969-   )

Joe-Pratt Blair = Sallie Lyles
(1963-   )   (1967-   )

Eppes   Lyles   Glenn
(1985-   )   (1986-   )   (2005-   )

stopher "Chris" = Nolee May Henderson
(1977-   )   (1980-   )

Henderson

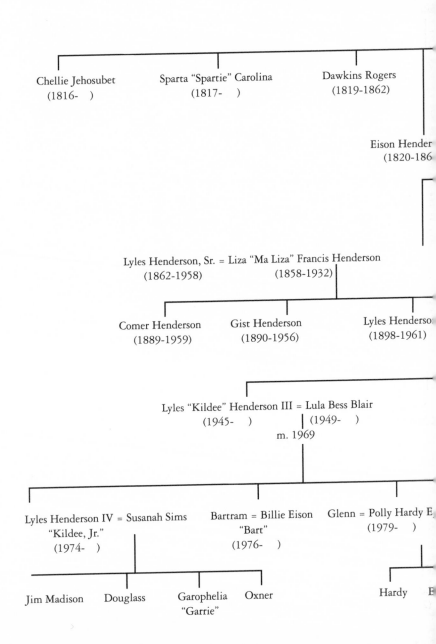

Chellie Jehosubet
(1816-)

Sparta "Spartie" Carolina
(1817-)

Dawkins Rogers
(1819-1862)

Eison Hender
(1820-186

Lyles Henderson, Sr. = Liza "Ma Liza" Francis Henderson
(1862-1958)   (1858-1932)

Comer Henderson
(1889-1959)

Gist Henderson
(1890-1956)

Lyles Henderso
(1898-1961)

Lyles "Kildee" Henderson III = Lula Bess Blair
(1945-)   (1949-)
m. 1969

Lyles Henderson IV = Susanah Sims
"Kildee, Jr."
(1974-)

Bartram = Billie Eison
"Bart"
(1976-)

Glenn = Polly Hardy E
(1979-)

Jim Madison   Douglass   Garophelia   Oxner
"Garrie"

Hardy   E

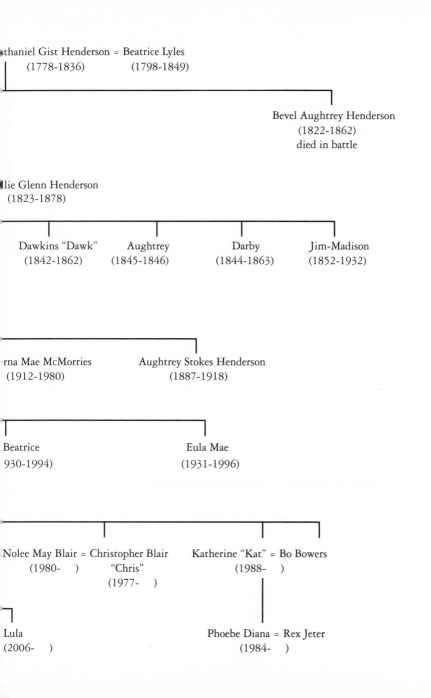

thaniel Gist Henderson = Beatrice Lyles
(1778-1836)   (1798-1849)

Bevel Aughtrey Henderson
(1822-1862)
died in battle

lie Glenn Henderson
(1823-1878)

| Dawkins "Dawk" | Aughtrey | Darby | Jim-Madison |
| (1842-1862) | (1845-1846) | (1844-1863) | (1852-1932) |

rna Mae McMorries   Aughtrey Stokes Henderson
(1912-1980)   (1887-1918)

Beatrice   Eula Mae
930-1994)   (1931-1996)

Nolee May Blair = Christopher Blair   Katherine "Kat" = Bo Bowers
(1980-)   "Chris"   (1988-)
                  (1977-)

Lula   Phoebe Diana = Rex Jeter
(2006-)   (1984-)